TH1

Producer & International Distributor
eBookPro Publishing
www.ebook-pro.com

The Jewish Priest: a novel
By Aaron Ben Shahar

Producer & International Distributor
eBookPro Publishing
www.ebook-pro.com
The Jewish Priest: a novel
Aaron Ben Shahar
Copyright © 2022 Aaron Ben Shahar

Translation: Sharon Singer
Contact: bsaaron28@gmail.com

ISBN 9798355803377

THE JEWISH PRIEST: A NOVEL

AARON BEN SHAHAR

PROLOGUE

July 22, 1946, Sayed remembered that day well. He had planned to approach the payphone in the lobby of the King David Hotel in Jerusalem and wait for a call from his parents in the late afternoon. They were supposed to arrive at a hotel in Khartoum, the capital of Sudan, and call him with greetings for his thirtieth birthday. He had no idea that the pleasant sunny day would end in disaster.

The echo of his footsteps were absorbed by the stone floor of the broad terrace of the King David hotel. Tall and proud, wearing a white galabia fastened by a draped gold belt and a blue turban on his head, he glided as a ghost among the white tablecloths and blue, delicately detailed oriental dinnerware. He had been doing it for years, ever since the manager of the hotel he worked at in Khartoum offered him and four others a job at the most luxurious hotel in Jesus' city, Jerusalem.

"They love Sudanese waiters there," the hotel manager explained to Sayed and his father, who came all the way from his small fishing village, calculating his recruitment commission in his head.

Once accepting the job offer in Jerusalem, he set off to say his goodbyes to his friends and family in the village of Kosti, located on a small island where the Blue and White Nile rivers met, north of Khartoum. His family and in fact, the entire village, were all anglers who thrived on the bounty from the White Nile for generations. Sayed was also meant to continue the family tradition along with his father and six older brothers until that one hot, humid day when his school principal summoned him and his father to a meeting and divulged that a relative of his from Khartoum needed an assistant chef at the hotel he ran and that naturally, he recommended Sayed, who he had always known as a talented and polite student.

Sayed was happy. Unlike his father and brothers, he felt there was more to life than tossing fishnets and sorting flapping fish into old crates. He had other aspirations and his father would not stand in his way. He had always hoped that one day, his youngest son would be a respectable man who would bring honor to his family. Therefore, shortly after the immediate response to the recruiter, Sayed was on his way to the grand hotel in Khartoum.

A few months after he began working, Sayed being a tall and handsome young man, was moved out of the kitchen and to the front of the house as a busser and thus began his career as a waiter. The stars were aligned, or perhaps it was simply that manager's quest for new recruits who would work in Jerusalem. Sayed, as we already know, understood the gravity of this opportunity and was eager to travel to the city of Jesus.

After he parted from his family and friends in a genuine display of emotion, he got on the ferry that cruised the Nile from Khartoum to Aswan in Egypt. Before he boarded, his contact handed him twenty guineas in disheveled bills to cover his expenses until he would arrive at the King David hotel in Jerusalem. He took the night train to Cairo from Aswan and from there, another twelve-hour train ride to Alexandria. He set sail to Jaffa, where he would get on a 'Diligence' stagecoach with his friends for another eight-hour journey. At some point, they would rest at the Turkish caravansary in Bab el-Wad. Once the horses perked up after their much-needed rest, the stagecoach continued to climb toward Jerusalem. Sayed and his buddies carried on by foot from the entrance to the city, directly to the King David.

From the moment it opened its doors in 1931, the chain of command at the King David was noticeably clear. The hotel manager was always English, the cooks Italian, and the waiters Sudanese. They were perfect for the job as they were tall, handsome, dedicated, and had a profound sense of hospitality that made them popular among patrons and guests.

The founders of the hotel were wealthy Jews from Egypt and Iraq, who intended for the hotel to deliver an exemplary first-class experience. The four and a half acre land they purchased from the Greek Orthodox church was left in the hands of capable architects with instructions to plan a unique and lavish hotel. Relishing the challenge, the designers built a hotel that word of its splendor reached everywhere across the Middle East.

A magnificent entrance led guests to a broad lobby on gleaming marble floors. Its walls were lined with walnut wood paneling, and from its high ceiling draped a unique chandelier attached to Carrara marble imported from Italy. The brass and crystal chandelier gave the hall even more grandeur and gentry. One hundred and twenty glass bulbs were mounted on its arms, and a customized mechanism enabled it to be lowered for maintenance and candle lighting on special occasions. Select artisans were brought in from Italy to decorate the lobby with dozens of embellishments inspired by Assyrian, Hittite, Phoenician, and Muslim cultures, as well as Jewish motifs starring the figures of Kings David and Solomon.

The six-story hotel's pièce de résistance was the east facing suites, offering a spectacular view of the old city. While most hotel guests would use the communal bathrooms at the end of the hallways as was customary in those days, the guests accommodated in the suites enjoyed their own private restrooms. Competition over the most significant wing of the hotel was won undoubtably by the dining room.

In the afternoons, the hotel lobby turned into the place to be for Jerusalem's high society. Sitting in the deep leather chairs pinned to thick Persian rugs were the wives of senior British officials, Jewish women who came to absorb the opulent atmosphere as well as other dignitaries visiting the city. The ladies would gather to chat while the men convened over a glass of fine whisky and a Cuban cigar to discuss Great Britain's stature in the Middle East, Arab-Jewish relations, and other matters of utmost importance.

The dining room was a culinary hotspot that served hotel guests and walk-ins alike. Breakfast was served in the form of a buffet. Bowls of delicacies from a selection of cuisines, from real Egyptian beans, through Russian caviar, to French omelets were all spread out on long tables covered with white tablecloths. The hotel bakery would work from late at night to indulge guests with a selection of fresh pastries, French baguettes, and pitas in a variety of shapes and flavors. Breakfast would end at around noon, and a team of waiters and cleaners would begin preparations for dinner service.

Dinner at the hotel was a festival of gastronomy and splendor. Admission to the Culinary Culture Hall was contingent on proper suits for men and evening gowns for women. During the war, British officers ranked Major and above were allowed to dine in their military uniform.

Waiters with at least ten years of experience, dressed in black, matching bow tie, and white gloves, served the guests courteously and skillfully. A dedicated waiter oversaw arranging the silverware and crystal plates placed on tables covered with mustard-colored tablecloths. The menu itself was printed on parchment paper and offered guests a selection of world-class delicacies. The Italian chef, second only to God, changed the menu daily.

Sayed and his friends from far-flung Khartoum arrived at the hotel. The very next day, before they could even recover from the rough journey, the hotel service manager, accompanied by the maître d', began to guide them through the ropes. After a week of intense training, a trainer was assigned to each Sudanese kid. The trainer was entrusted with their trainee's integration in the relevant departments. Two young men were sent to serve as dinner service assistant waiters, two were designated to work the breakfast service, and Sayed was assigned to the terrace.

Sayed loved the broad round terrace, paved with red Hebron stone, and a railing made of crafted rectangular stones. It was in the eastern part of the hotel, and it had a direct entrance from the lobby. In its northern section, there was a wide staircase where one could go down to the swimming pool and the magnificent garden.

The glory of the terrace was in the remarkable view it provided. Some would say that it was one of the three most beautiful landscapes in the world. To the east, you could see the old city walls where the Tower of David protruded from. South of the walls saw Mount Zion and its many towers and palaces. Beyond the wall, the domes of the old city emerged like a bed of mushrooms in a magical forest. And above all stood out the Dome of the Rock like a painting of a fairy tale; and not far from there, the dome of Al-Aqsa Mosque rounded up to the sky. As a backdrop to it all, rested the Mount of Olives and its holiness hovering around it.

The terrace and the luncheons served there were Sayed's realm, without a doubt. Attentive and dedicated to his work, he floated between the tables seeking to read the eyes of his guests for their needs and before it reached their lips. True to the waiter's oath (of those days, anyway) not to engage in any gossip, in the few conversations with his parents in Sudan, he never discussed the guests he had the opportunity to host on the terrace. Such guests would including British Colonial Minister Winston Churchill, Lord Edmund Allenby, the Kings of Spain and Greece, Emir Abdullah of Jordan, and the Emperor of Ethiopia, Haile Selassie, who had made the King David Hotel his permanent residence while in exile.

In 1938, the British leased the southern wing of the hotel and made it the administrative center of the British

Mandate in Palestine. In addition, they rented an entire row of rooms reserved for distinguished British guests. One of the regular guests was a tall Englishman who Sayed knew nothing about except for his name – David. He had appeared at the hotel in the end of WWII and made the southern wing his residence.

One day the Englishman went down to the lobby, where the hotel's customer service manager was waiting, and after a short chat, the manager called Sayed over.

"David is asking for a single table on the terrace, could you arrange that for him?" he asked.

Sayed nodded and asked David to accompany him, not before the hotel manager whispered in his ear, "VIP treatment."

Without any hesitation, Sayed led his guest to the southern part of the terrace, to a more secluded area where a beautiful Damascus-style wooden table stood, adorned with animal carvings, and two armchairs upholstered in red cashmere, one on each side. Sayed knew that his guest would love that corner, as it was his own favorite. From the alcove one could control everything going on across the terrace, while safeguarding the intimate setting guests expected. The terrace had yet another advantage. In the early afternoon, the southern wing of the hotel cast a pleasant shadow, which provided an adequate solution for sweltering summer days that would sometimes plague Jerusalem.

David would adopt that spot. Every day at quarter to noon, he would take his place by the Damascus table.

Handsome, tall, broad-shouldered, short black hair, and brown-eyed David had Sayed curious.

This man is playing some sort of game, he thought to himself and immediately recalled the oath he took and shook away those reflections.

There were days when the Englishman, as Sayed named him in his mind, would sit in a gray three-piece suit and a pocket watch at the end of a chain that started attached to his belt and ended in the front pocket of his trousers, just like the perfect English gentleman. Other days, he would surprise Sayed wearing a pristine uniform of a heavily decorated British Army Major, and a peaked cap adorned with two golden ribbons.

One day, Sayed noticed a man wearing a black robe sitting at David's table, all on his own. As he pondered as to how he would ask him to clear the table, he approached and discovered that beneath the long priest's robe was no other than David himself. A belt was tied around his waist and a gleaming bronze necklace hung over his chest and the large silver cross at its end indicated his honorable standing.

Sayed, who over the years had learned never to be shocked by anything, was not able to wipe off the puzzled look on his face. David's face, however, did not move a muscle.

"The usual," he said and sank into the Times newspaper he was holding.

Many guests frequented David's table. Englishmen, Arabs, Jews, including English people in civilian clothes, rabbis, Christian clergymen, Arab imams, and other figures representing the human tapestry of Palestine.

Curiosity is the waiter's enemy, Sayed reminded himself as he fulfilled his duties faithfully and was never hurt when people at the table would stop talking as he approached. "Too bad the cutlery has no ears," he mumbled to himself in moments of weakness and quickly acted just like the mute tableware.

At noon most of the tables would be empty, nevertheless Sayed knew that at one o'clock, when British officials broke off from their work, the terrace would fill up. At exactly a quarter to twelve David took to his table. Soon after, Sayed noticed a tall priest in a crimson robe standing at the entrance, with a round hood of the same color, and a large copper cross dangling from his chest. When Sayed noticed that the guest was looking for someone on the terrace, he did not hesitate and immediately led the priest directly to David's table.

When he noticed the guest, David stood up, spread his arms open and they both fell into each other's arms.

Sayed, who knew David as a cold man who had never shown any emotion, was surprised by the reaction the meeting evoked. He stepped back so as not to disturb the intimacy between the two.

David saw Sayed's discomfort and turned to him with a smile. "This is the most precious person in the world to me!"

Sayed almost fainted. It was the first complete personal sentence he had heard from David in all the years of their acquaintance. Excited, he rushed to the kitchen, grabbed a jug of water and with a slight bow placed it on the table. The cool water was pumped from a private well dug in the hotel garden, and its quality waters quenched the thirst of its guests.

"The usual?" Sayed asked.

David nodded. "And the same for my guest." Immediately adding in a slight authoritative tone, "But take into account, Sayed, that we are short on time here."

Sayed hastened to place the order and even served them, at their request, glasses of beer – two cups each. It was a quarter past twelve.

"We're in a hurry, but I promised Sam we would not leave without taking a bite out of our trifle," David said.

"I didn't need much convincing... the truth is that I came here solely because word of the trifle you serve here has made its way all the way to London," the guest replied smiling and Sayed puffed out his chest with immense pride.

"But it's going to take a quarter of an hour. You know we don't have a trifle ready as we only make it to order," Sayed said.

"The goal justifies the time," the guest replied with a sigh, glancing at his watch.

The King David Trifle was a brand in its own right, known everywhere, from Cairo to Beirut. The famous English dessert received an upgrade at the hotel, and all would talk in its praise. A secret recipe for cooked fruit mixed tartlets, fresh bananas and sweet cream, colorful jelly with strips of yellow custard and other special secrets are what made it. Fans of the delicacy had sworn that to make this smashing dessert, the hotel management had to have stolen the sweets from Windsor Palace, no less.

Sayed often asked himself how the guests would react if they knew that the royal trifle was prepared by Fatima, the Arab cook from the village of Ein Karem. An English nun taught her how to make it at the convent adjacent to her village, where she worked for many years.

At twelve thirty minus fifteen seconds Sayed stood in front of the kitchen counter just as Fatima sprinkled Belgian chocolate crumbs on both plates. He took them as a skilled waiter in one hand, placed a starched white napkin on the other, and rushed to the south table with a skilled smile, as he noticed the priest coming out of the bathroom and walking behind him.

As he stepped onto the terrace, the floor shook. Flames rose from the hotel, stones flew, as one hit his head. Waves of black soot enveloped the terrace and scattered shards of glass covered its floor. His white turban was gone, and his white galabia was blackened to the last of its threads.

True to the waiter's oath, Sayed tried to fulfill his mission. Instinctively, he covered the two plates that miraculously remained intact and groped his way in the dark to the south table.

He was completely dumbfounded as he saw that the entire southern section of the terrace and the table with it looked like it was severed with a scalpel.

David had also disappeared, as if he were swallowed by the earth.

Sayed stopped at the end of what was once a beautiful terrace, right on the edge of a gaping abyss. Everything was covered in fire and clouds of smoke. His head was spinning, his breathing heavy.

Before collapsing into a lucky black out, he heard behind him the priest's cry, "Brother, my brother..."

He did not hear the howls of the Red Cross ambulances and police sirens rushing to the devastated hotel that came shortly after.

CHAPTER 1 – YESODOT

The farmers of the small village were rejoicing. The synagogue was finally open after a long wait from when they decided to build one when they first broke ground. The synagogue had foremost importance to the community, not only as a house of prayer but mostly as a heritage site, a reminder of the lives they left in Romania for the sake of starting anew in the land of Israel.

Located south of lake Hahula the village was built on both sides of its main and only road that ended at an allotment designated for a synagogue. The small village bungalows attested to the settlers' financial state, who worked so hard to make ends meet though skimmed none when it came to the synagogue.

The synagogue was designed by a well-known Haifa-based architect, Abu Khoury, who funnily enough, made a name for himself designing Jewish temples. He chose to build the synagogue from a particular stone brought in by a camel caravan from Hebron. The front door was built using special beech wood brought in from Lebanon, and above the entrance right in the center was a small square with a Star of David composed of a colorful mosaic. The stone-paved main hall of the synagogue, was wide enough to accommodate all the villagers and more, hinting of the days to come when the population would grow.

The hall had two rows of benches spaced apart. This was a compromise between those who were stricter, advocating for a separation between men and women and the majority of the villagers who were content with simply adhering to the prohibition of touching between genders.

In the center of the synagogue was a cedar Torah arc, which was attached to the eastern wall of the synagogue. In front of the ark hung a white curtain that separated the space of the synagogue from the Torah scroll. It was made of white silk with embroidery of the seven-branched menorah and the symbols of the twelve tribes of Israel around it.

The Torah scroll had a story of its own. Abraham, one of the village elders, donated it willingly after bringing it with him from Ploieşti, Romania, where his family resided for many generations. According to family history, the scroll itself was written in Spain and went with the family since its exile from Spain in the late 15th century. The hidden scroll was covered with silver embellishments to which the donor added a bronze plaque: "In memory of my parents, Yehuda and Dina, who never made it to the land of Israel."

Adjacent to the synagogue, they built a small building with a kitchenette, a toilet, and a warehouse to serve worshipers, and another room for the council to convene.

After the inauguration of the magnificent building in the presence of all the residents, the committee convened on that and decided to appoint a permanent rabbi, since just as there is no Torah scroll without a crown, there is no synagogue without a rabbi.

In another meeting, a chairperson nominated Rabbi Shlomo as the village rabbi after hearing from his in-laws about a brilliant student from one of the leading Yeshivas in Safed, who was ordained as a rabbi and was searching for a place where he could combine Torah with crafts. Rumor had it that the distinguished rabbi who was well versed in Torah and mitzvas, was known as one who was strict where he must and lenient when he could afford.

Shlomo, or His Honor, arrived at the village with his young wife, Hannah, and their two sons, Shmuel and David.

They were given a house to live in, and at Hannah's request a piece of land, as did the other villagers. Not many days passed, and the couple had a baby girl. Unfortunately, that was the couple's last pregnancy that would bear children. Shlomo accepted the decree calmly. This is the will of God, he said to himself. Even an all-azure tallit as his wife, sometimes bore a blemish. As she was born on Purim, they named their daughter Esther.

Shlomo loved his work and loved the people. His kind face and life wisdom brought people closer to the synagogue. Every evening, even on weekdays and despite the arduous work, a quorum of worshipers gathered for the evening prayers. After that, he would return home, eat dinner with his family, and continue his studies and reflection, as written in the scriptures: "and you shall contemplate in it day and night."

One week a year, the rabbi traveled to the city of Safed, mingled in ancient synagogues, and drew all he could from Kabbalah and Jewish mysticism. On the following week he would go to Jerusalem, hopping between yeshivas to hear the latest on Halacha innovations and the rulings of the great arbitrators.

**

There was no doubt that the words to "A Woman of Valor, who will Find" were written about Hannah. She gave her husband the respect and status and left running matters of home and family to herself. She made sure to address him as Your Honor and taught her children to do the same when they were in public. Only in more lighter situations would they call him "Dad." She would reserve the name "Shlomi" only for intimate settings between the two.

The kitchen was in the center of their small home. On the wooden counter, Hannah placed a primus stove next to a kerosene cooker and a set of pots and cookware she had gotten in the market in Tiberius. Under the window facing out to the backyard, she had built a cooler cabinet to keep groceries fresh. The kitchen had running water from a pipe connected to a water tank that rested on wooden boards outside the house. Twice a week, the village council would send a cart strapped to a mule carrying a large silo of water so that water would be pumped manually into the house.

Every evening, after washing their hands and blessing their food, the honorable rabbi would sit at the head of the table with his wife and children, to eat the meal Hannah labored to prepare. Later, the rabbi would discuss biblical law after which the children would retire to their rooms to do their homework, while the rabbi continued his studies and Hannah with her demanding daily routine.

In a small lounge past the kitchen the honorable rabbi would see visitors who would not normally frequent the synagogue or preferred to meet him in a less formal environment. By the fireplace stood a pile of firewood for the frigid winter days and near it, "the trap," which was a clay bowl rubbed with carob honey and filled with pungent wild herbs. The trap was meant to protect from the Anopheles mosquito that would live in the swamps that surrounded the nearby lake. The pungent smells that rose from the bowl would attract the mosquitos and they would get stuck to the honey. Once a week, Hannah would clean the bowl of all the dead mosquitos and change its contents. All were fearful of Malaria, known also as "swamp fever," which brought about the death of many residents at the time.

One bedroom was for the parents while the other housed the three children. When Esther grew up, her parents built her a small room of her own, and when Shmuel went off to study in a Yeshiva in Jerusalem, Dudi was left with a room to himself, counting his blessings.

The toilet was outside. It consisted of a whole in the ground topped with a wooden seat, surrounded by walls made of reeds brought from the lake. When the pit was full, it would be covered in dirt and the seat and walls moved to another pit that was dug nearby. During the chilly winter days, the family would do their business in a tin pot that stood by the door. The next morning, it would be emptied out in the pit outside. The shower was also built in the yard out of reeds, under the open sky. The floor was made of stones covered in a Cyperus mat. The water reached the shower through a thin hose extended from the house. Whenever anyone would want to wash their body with hot water, they would have to heat the water using the primus in the kitchen and then carry the water out to the shower in a large pot.

Like most village houses, the cottage was painted white and covered with red slates imported from a factory in Marseilles, France. A path paved with loam soil led from the house to the main and only street in the village. At the end of the path grew Sky Duster trees, whose slender trunk proudly boasted a canopy of branches rising to the sky, followed by colorful flowerbeds adorning both its sides. Behind the flowerbeds lay a vegetable and herb garden that was cultivated by Hannah, providing for most of the family's needs. Past the vegetable garden, there were almond and apple trees that in the spring would drape the house in a white, fragrant gown.

In the back, close enough to smell, was the family dairy farm that would be empty from time to time as its tenants would regularly be out grazing in the pasture, except for Matilda, who two days earlier was bit by a snake. Ali, the good shepherd saved her life. He dressed her wound with a mixture of venom-repellant herbs and suggested she stay in the stall for recovery.

***

A year into Shlomo's tenure as rabbi of the village, swarms of locust ravaged all crops, trees, and pastureland. The farmers' dire financial state made it hard enough as it was to pay the rabbi's modest salary.

Hannah would not give up easily. Trying to prevent imminent famine, she traveled to Safed and Tiberias where she could ask family and friends for help. Yet, the sense of humiliation that enveloped and scorched her soul led her to pledge: No More.

Upon her return, she put up a fence and procured a cow. She made a quick work of learning how to dairy farm and soon managed to acquire yet another cow, realizing she had quite a knack for the trade. Everything she touched would turn into pearls. She churned butter, cultured cheese, skimmed milk all with formidable talent. Her now six cows cooperated and as a reward for her excellent care, they provided an abundance of milk. At the advice of a good friend from the large adjacent village of Rosh Pina, Hannah made and sold cheese to her neighbors and at times to residents of Rosh Pina and even Safed.

The daily care was entrusted in the capable hands of Ali, who lived in the Mud Village on the muddy banks of the lake. It was nicknamed "mud village" as it was built upon the swamps that expanded and shrank according to season.

Mud dwellers such as members of Ali's family earned their keep by weaving mats from Cyperus branches that grew abundantly on the lake shore and grazing water buffalos plucked into enclosures from the large wild herds. The local farmers' income was quite meager, therefore, Ali was happy to accept offers by villagers to help oversee their barns.

Each morning at dawn, Ali would go from one dairy farm to the next, open the gates and take the cows, who were glad to see him, out to graze. At the end of each day, right before sunset, he would return to the village, leading the cows behind him like the piper from that old story. Each cow that had eaten her fill, would show herself into her own stall.

One morning, he was approached by Hannah, who by then was a certified dairy farmer who owned six cows.

"What are we going to do, Ali?" she asked. "The cheeses are doing well, but I don't have enough milk."

Ali scratched his head in thought and then said, "I have an idea. We have water buffalo shepherds in our tribe. The buffalo don't produce much milk and the little they do you don't seem to like. It is quite possible that what is not good for drinking might be good for producing cheese."

Hannah liked the idea and ordered a trial batch of water buffalo milk from Ali.

***

Later that night, Hannah sat in the corner of the kitchen exhausted from working all day, with a long face. Her husband was sitting across from her, leaning over one of his holy books.

"Tell me, Shlomi," she addressed him somewhat worried. "Can I ask you a question?"

Shlomi lifted his head with worry as he knew that when she needed something from him, she would call him "Shlomi."

"Yes, yes," he responded impatiently.

"Is water buffalo kosher or not?"

The honorable rabbi's glasses slid down to the tip of his nose.

They had a tacit understanding between them: he did not bother her with trivial questions related to housekeeping or livelihood, and she did not bother him with sacred questions such as what is the fate of a red cow that ate grass on Yom Kippur.

"Why are you asking? You are the second person this week who has come to me with this question."

"Who else asked?" she asked with a frown.

"Zalman, the butcher from Rosh Pina," he replied.

"And what was your answer?" she asked, relaxing a little.

"I checked and found that the water buffalo chews cud, is cloven hoofed, and its milk coagulates. Besides, our ancestors used to eat its meat. The conclusion is that it is kosher." The rabbi put his glasses back on and returned to the issue of the red cow.

Hannah slept well that night. She dreamed of red water buffalos and white cows.

The next morning, Ali appeared on a gray donkey carrying a clay jug on each side. "I have some water buffalo milk for you," he said. "You should know that this is milk with higher concentrations of fat than what you are used to."

He had come just in time. The cows' milk she milked herself and bought from her neighbors was not enough for the amount of cheese and butter she had planned to make. In the afternoon, after finishing her daily tasks, Hannah turned to a large copper pot resting on the wood stove in the garden. She filled part of it with water buffalo milk and added double what she had milked from her cows, lit the wood, and turned the fire up. The hot fire brought the milk to a quick boil. At that point, she poured a dash of vinegar into the milk, added pinches of herbs that had grown in her garden while stirring the white liquid with a large wooden spoon.

Several minutes later, she removed the pot from the stove and placed it on a reed mat. She poured the milk into a cloth diaper and tightened its contents over a bucket. After the liquids had drained into the bucket, she salted the curd, tied the diaper back up using Cyperus rope and hung it over a wooden beam, leaving it to the chill of the night to do its work.

At dawn, before the rest of the family woke up and went about their day, she rushed to the garden, took down the cold cloth diaper, opened it and poured its contents into a big wooden bowl that sat on the wooden table in the yard. The curd slid right into it, and she let it harden. All that remained for her was to taste. The texture of the cheese was pleasant and the flavor deep and slightly sour redolent of herbs and the water of the Jordan river.

Hannah sliced the wheel of cheese into wedges, packing each in a Cyperus leaves wrapper prepared for her by the elderly Bedouin women from the swamp. She sent the cheese wedges off with the daily carriage that travelled from the village to Rosh Pina and on to Safed to Old Man Rosenfeld's specialty cheese shop that was well-known throughout the Galilee.

That day, she was in for a surprise. In the afternoon, after milking and before going back into the house to get settled for dinner, she noticed someone in the yard, on a brown mule. It was no other than Old Man Rosenfeld. He was nicknamed that as according to local gossip, he had long passed the age of sixty. She had known Rosenfeld for years. At first, she would go to his shop every Shavuot holiday to buy special cheeses, and once she began to make her own, she was so proud that Rosenfeld agreed to sell the cheese wedges she would send to his shop every few days.

The surprising visit stunned Hannah so much, she almost dropped the two buckets of milk she was hauling. Rosenfeld, who saw her excitement, grabbed the buckets before they could fall to the ground and invited himself in.

"Tea or milk?" she asked and calmed down a little as he sat at the kitchen table.

"The cobbler walks barefoot, and a dairy farmer doesn't drink milk." He smiled.

Hannah, who kept water in a kettle on the wood stove, poured the boiling water into a large glass she kept in the vitrine for special occasions, added tea extract, two teaspoons of brown sugar, and a wedge of a lemon that grew on a tree in the front. She placed the tea close to her guest along with two homemade sesame cookies and waited to hear what he had to say.

"What cheese was that you sent today with Gershon the coachman?" he asked.

"It's something new I tried today," she answered.

"You must give me the recipe. It is the best cheese I have had in years."

Hannah wiped her hands on the kitchen towel hanging on the chair, poured him another cup of tea, and nudged him to nibble on the cookies.

"I can't give you the recipe, but I'd be happy to sell you more of my cheeses."

"I knew you wouldn't give me the recipe." He sighed. "But promise me you will send me a lot of those wedges." He parted with her affably and rushed to Rosh Pina to meet other associates.

Hannah's business expanded. "Hannah's Cheeses" became quite popular. The amount of water buffalo milk she would purchase from Ali kept growing and she would pay a Bedouin girl Ali had recommended to collect herbs for her around the swamp and on the slopes of the surrounding hills. The herbs would give "Hannah's Cheeses" their unique, exotic flavors. As her business grew, Ali's cousin brought six tin milk cans he purchased for her at Ali's recommendation in the flea market in Damascus.

One day, a man appeared in her yard, which at that point had become a small dairy farm, a respectable man who introduced himself as Monsieur Curie. Just like any self-respecting cheesemaker at the time, Hannah was familiar with the name. "Curie et fils – fromagerie française" was a large cheese and herb business in Haifa. His customers included the high-ranking Ottoman officials who would buy considerable amounts of cheese he would import from France especially for them.

"I have tasted your cheeses," he told Hannah. "And I would like to sell them in France. A ship from France will be arriving in Haifa in two weeks. We could send the cheeses back with it. I think that you and I could do good business there." He smiled and soon left.

Days later, she had ten wheels of cheese, in various textures thanks to the different ratios between cow and water buffalo milk as well as the herbs she used. Now, all that was needed was for her to send her culinary creations to Monsieur Curie in Haifa.

CHAPTER 2 – DUDI

The honorable rabbi had cracked many complicated questions, though one remained unresolved: How did he and Hannah manage to produce two quite different sons. They were like fire and water; black and white; shadow and light.

Shmuel, the elder was the smart, disciplined, serious one who would listen to his father with utmost reverence. He was average height and brown eyes. In school, his teachers predicted he would be a great Torah scholar. In his spare time, he would sit at his father's feet at the synagogue and thirstily gulped his sermons and commentaries on the Torah. Deep down in her heart, his mother hoped that he would follow in his father's footsteps and that he would be ordained rabbi and perhaps become the rabbi of Rosh Pina. His father, too, saw he was meant for greatness. He believed with all his heart his son could one day be the head of a Yeshiva.

When Shmuel tuned six, his father enrolled him in a cheider,[1] as early preparation for the career awaiting him. Indeed, at the age of fourteen he was accepted to a

---

1. **Cheider** is a traditional elementary school for boys teaching the basics of Judaism and Hebrew.

prestigious yeshiva in Jerusalem and climbed the scholarly ranks. The separation from his parents made it difficult for Shmuel and so did the separation from his younger brother, Dudi, and Esther, his beautiful little sister. But faithful to his father's word and imbued with the sense of mission according to which he was educated, he did not hesitate too much before moving to Jerusalem.

Dudi, as his friends called him was a tall, dark, and handsome boy. The adoring eyes of the village girls would constantly follow him around. He loved to learn yet disliked school. In one of his bible classes at school when the teacher linked the reeds that grew by the swamps to the stories of the Torah, Dudi jumped right out of his chair.

"Rush and reed are not the same thing!" he yelled. "Those are two different shrubs."

The teacher was surprised both by Dudi's rare contribution to the class and by his audacity to contradict him.

"How dare you undermine me?" he scoffed.

After the break was over, the teacher did not find Dudi back in class, however, on the blackboard, in big letters, he found the words:

"Reed and rush shall decay"
Isaiah 19:6

One day, Dudi noticed a donkey wandering in the fields with fallen ears, long eyelashes covering his sad eyes, and his body dirty and faded. He found two torn sacks and made them into rope, which he then tied around the donkey's neck. He led him to the family's property and tied him to the marvelous oak tree. He then brought a bucket of cold water and watered the donkey, who was so thirsty that he feared he could drink the bucket as well.

Dudi washed and scrubbed his skin until his original white color was revealed and offered him a heap of hay. It took him but seconds to name him "Balaam," after a biblical master of a donkey, or a jenny, to be precise. That afternoon, Dudi invited his brother, who in those days was still living in the village, to meet Balaam.

"I offer you a partnership in this donkey," he said.

Love indeed prevailed between the brothers even though they did not always see eye to eye. Shmuel despised rebelliousness, and Dudi did not appreciate surrendering to conventions.

"But what does that mean?" Shmuel asked.

"Just as we share a room and our clothes, we will share the donkey as partners. We can ride him to Rosh Pina, and you can take him to the cheider."

Shmuel gaped at his brother in shock and asked, "Do you know what my teacher will do to me?! And besides, who will clean after him?"

Right in front of them, the donkey defecated on the straw.

"Fifty-fifty" Dudi replied.

"No, thank you." Shmuel hastened to decline his brother's generous offer.

When the rabbi heard about his son's new friend, he turned angrily to his wife. "What would the rabbi's son be doing with an unclean beast?" he huffed. "He should join me at the synagogue like Shmuel does, instead of messing around with a donkey."

"Leave him be," Hannah replied, smiling inside. "He will bring honor to you and the people of Israel, you'll see."

Several days later, Hannah was asked to an urgent meeting with the school principal. She went to the meeting without her husband.

"Such a pleasure to meet you," said the principal. "I didn't want to bother the rabbi, so I asked to see you instead."

"What is the matter?" she asked.

"I wanted to tell you that this time, Dudi went too far. He came into the school on the back of a white donkey and when the gym teacher asked him what he thought he was doing, his response was that he was the Messiah."

Hannah's face dropped.

"We have decided not to expel him for now," he assured her. "A three-day suspension will do."

Hannah loved Dudi with all her heart. He was the embodiment of all the dreams she knew she would never fulfil herself. She admired his creativity, his love of nature, his curiosity, and love of life that burst out of him, and the more the rabbi came to terms with the fact that he would never be a great Torah scholar, the more her love for him grew.

Later that afternoon, she called to him and said, "I met with the principal today and he said that you told one of your teachers that you were the Messiah."

"No, I didn't!" Dudi replied. "I told him that the donkey looks like that of the Messiah's."

Hannah did not know if she should laugh or cry. "If I were to tell your father about this, he would lock you in the storage room for three days. But I have an idea… since you don't have school now, perhaps you could help me deliver cheese to Monsieur Curie in Haifa."

She trusted her son with that task.

Three were happy with this trip to Haifa: Dudi who avoided being locked up in the storage room, his mother who was given the chance of a lifetime to sell cheese to "Curie et fils," and Curie *sans ses* fils, who believed in the uniqueness of Hannah's cheeses and relished the opportunity to show the proud French that good cheese was being produced in the land of Jesus as well.

Monsieur Curie was happy to receive the delivery and told Dudi that he would settle the bill with his mother. Since he was late for the last Diligence ride from Haifa to

Safed, the French gentleman suggested he spend the night in the Anglican church nearby.

"Don't worry, they only charge a Mil per night," assured Monsieur Curie.

The following day, Dudi took the Diligence to Safed and from there made his way home through Rosh Pina. The three suspension days passed and Dudi would never return to school.

***

Lake Hahula was Dudi's home. Whenever he had free time, he would head down the gravel trail from the outskirts of the village through the almond orchards and herb gardens to the lake. On his way, Dudi would cross through overgrown reeds that seemed taller as he neared the lake.

On one of his walks, he heard rattling sounds and noticed a large black wild boar walking in front of him at arm's length. She crossed the trail and behind her, four little piglets were keeping eye contact with her curly tail. After the family had disappeared in the undergrowth, Dudi set his gaze toward where she popped out and noticed a narrow, winding trail in the wild. He began to walk the winding path and the closer he got to the lake, the higher the reeds reached until they would hide the sunlight.

Dudi almost yielded to the weight of the mud on his feet and thought to head back when the shadow of a giant tree grabbed his attention. He walked a few feet further and reached an enchanted world. A broad oak tree grew on the bank of the lake; its top wide and trunk divided into all directions like snakes.

Dudi sat on one of the offshoots and looked around. Stretched before him was a peaceful, blue lake. The water was dotted with Nymphaea, white and azure-like little pieces of sky that had fallen down to the water and colorful fireflies sunbathing on the floating vegetation. Every now and again, a tilapia would peek its head as it tried to hunt for lunch over one of the leaves. The riverbank was home to a variety of aquatic herbs, namely the yellow Water Lily.

One could constantly hear songbirds, even when a swamp cat would snarl. A vibrant bee eater was perched on a branch in anticipation of a small fish to be tempted to get a closer look at the bright colors above the water. The picturesque scenery was hypnotic. The volcanic Golan heights rose from the east while the soft evergreen mountains of the Galilee spread through the west. Overlooking it all was Mount Hermon and its snowy peak that glowed under the warm sun.

Happy and elated, Dudi soaked in the intoxicating sights and scents. Sitting on the tree trunk, he let his mind and his soul merge with the wonderous site he discovered thanks to the wild boar. When he realized the hour was getting late, he got up and walked back to the village, not wanting to worry his mother any more than she should have.

"Don't you ever go there," was the first sentence every good village mother would have instructed her children. "People there are dirty and diseased," they would say. That was a clear enough order for Dudi to disobey. As a child, he would sneak away "there" and would be completely captivated by what he saw: huts planted on the muddy riverbanks known to the privy few as the "Mud Village."

Dwellers were farmers, descendants of the Hourani tribe from the township of Da'el in southern Syria. To strengthen their grip over the Hahula lake area, with one hundred Turkish Lira, the local Ottoman government persuaded the head of the village to send farmers to live south of the lake in return for plenty of land for them to work and live. The naïve villagers and their slightly less gullible leader accepted the offer and moved down to the lake.

At first, they felt encouraged the fertile green land and the water buffalo herds grazing by waters were different to the solid, dry terrain, and blistering sun of southern Syria. But then came winter. During the sweltering summer days, the lake would stretch down the valley like an azure pearl earring, while its waters reflected the Golan Heights in the morning and the shadows of the Galilee hilltops in the afternoon. A narrow creek carved its way through the Basalt, winding and flowing into the Sea of Galilee. In the winter, water flowed from the Jordan River's streams overflooding the lake and much of its surroundings, thus tripling its size and earning it the nickname "The Inflating Lake."

The first winter introduced the farmers to the hardships of the wetlands. Much to their dismay, they would wake up to rising waters and their tents being washed away. Only with the arrival of spring did the marsh drain into the Jordan and flush into the Sea of Galilee. Learning their lesson, the villagers shook off the winter sludge and built a dirt levee separating them from the lake. They built permanent homes from mud bricks, covering their roofs with warp and weft reeds.

The farmers made their living growing rice and wheat in the fields around them, alas the peat would allow for only modest yields. As time went by, they learned to develop a reciprocal relationship with the large herds of water buffalo, the kings of the lake. These were large beasts, an upgraded cow of a sort. For hours, they would sit in the water before they would come out to graze around the lake. From time to time, the farmers would isolate a herd, earning their trust with a steady supply of fresh weeds. In return, the buffalo would allow the farmers to milk the females. A female water buffalo would give very little yet high in fat milk.

The villagers did not need much as it were, and they would dilute the fat with water from one of the nearby streams.

As the old Arab saying goes, "Give time some time, and with time experience will come."

Indeed, life experience and their meager livelihood taught the villages to make the most out of the rich foliage around them. The tall reeds, which would reach upward of sixteen feet, undoubtably ruled the area. The abundant water and summer heat provided it with ideal growing conditions. Local dwellers would chop the reeds, remove the leaves, and dry them over mud pallets that would harden in the sun. These would serve as roofs and fences for their homes. For bricks, they turned to the abundance of mud, as their attempts to make the walls of their homes out of reeds failed, as written in the scriptures: "That splintered reed of a staff, which enters and punctures the palm of anyone who leans on it."

The dried reeds were designated for trade. In the summer, when the marshlands would dry and the roads would open, the villagers would haul it on camels through various towns as far as Tiberius. During the spring, the reeds would boast hairy inflorescences that, from a distance, resembled flags at the top of their masts. The women would chop the flowerings and use them to sweep their floors. When times were hard, and there were many, the women would extract the core of the roots and cook them slowly in clay ovens located by each hut. When cooked long enough, the root would taste almost like a potato.

Cooking was the women's domain. Made out of dry mud rectangular bricks, the bottoms of the ovens were lined with dry bulrush that would grow among the reeds, topped with reeds and wood chips from trees that grew on the hilltops. The dry bulrush was lit by rubbing together basalt stones brought down from the volcanic hills of the Golan.

The reeds were a good audience, nevertheless the undisputed king of the marshlands was the Cyperus. It grew in the water and its crown-wearing highpoints seemed to almost loathe the hairy crassness of the reeds. Among the various species of Cyperus in the lake grew the papyrus, which earned its place in history thanks to the ancient Egyptian hieroglyphics written on paper made from the pith of the plant. Cyperus was used until the invention of the press by Gutenberg in the 15th century yet at that time, Cyperus was common mainly in Sudan as well as Lake Hahula.

Cyperus was loved especially by the women who would chop it down it while the men split the reeds. At the end of each rainy season, the women would follow the receding waters toward the Cyperus fields, charged with energies they harbored during the months of isolation forced upon them by the heavy siege of muddy waters. Trudging through the mire that had yet to fully dry, they marched together, scythes in hand.

The piles were fanned out on clay beds for the branches to dry out. These were later used to make mats, houseware items, shoes, baskets, rope, and wide-brimmed hats that provided protection from the scorching sun. Once they would finish their arduous work, the men would load their wives' harvest onto wide-hoofed camels and delivered them to merchants in Rosh Pina and Safed. The merchants, who knew of the plight of the mud village dwellers, paid them pennies for the goods and sometimes simply traded them for flour, salt, and other basic supplies, which would prove necessary during the besieging winter.

***

On one glorious spring day when the world appeared as a child's innocent drawing – the blue skies competing with the color of the lake, the green mountains, and the white peak of the Hermon, Dudi went down the path that extended from the village to the lake. A few feet before the path would meet the water, he turned right into the mud village. The path itself would turn into a marsh in winter yet when summer neared, the water would retreat, and the scorching heat would transform the muck into solid ground.

Two buildings differed from the other mud huts. One boasted a blue dome topped with a silver crescent while the other was Suliman's large home. Dudi got to know Suliman totally by chance.

One spring day, when the water began to recede, Dudi decided to visit the village. He marched down the main boulevard careful not to slip into the puddles left by the retreating lake when he noticed a different house from the rest. It was not the size that intrigued Dudi but rather the boat tied to a post in front of the house, swaying in the water. The wooden boat was simple and seemed to have originated in the woods that grew around the lake. Two oars were looped to it with their grips in the air and their wide blades sunken in the quiet water.

Dudi was mostly curious about the boat and there, all of a sudden, appeared a tall man who had to tilt his head in order to walk through the house's low lintel. His white beard sloped down his chest, matching the pure white galabia he was wearing, which was a contrast to the muddy brown color that prevailed in the village.

"Come in," the old man said to Dudi.

Dudi was surprised by the invitation but even more so, to hear Hebrew come out of his host's mouth. The floor was covered in mats painted in unusual colors. In the corner of the room was a stove connected to a chimney made of mud bricks. The ceiling was built using wooden beams that bore the dry reeds and wedged bulrush for insulation. By the stove was a bed made out of wood, covered with a vibrant quilt, and right next to it a large clay bowl that gave a potent scent of sage. The surrounding walls were paneled with rows of reeds in various heights. A large wooden table took up most of the room and next to it, a vivid armchair with armrests made of wood and covered in braded colorful beads that mesmerized Dudi with their beauty and exoticness. Set out on the table was Cyperus spread out in various lengths and right beside them a bowl with different sized knives and a wooden mug holding stationery. Dudi recognized black and white of a porcupine that fed many families in the marshland.

The host was happy about his visitor and welcomed him graciously, "My name is Suliman. And what is yours?"

"My name is Dudi. What do you do with all of this Cyperus?"

Suliman loved Dudi's curiosity. Not many showed much interest in his craft. "I create sheets of papyrus and write on them," he replied. "You must have heard of hieroglyphics. Ancient Egyptian wise men would write on papyrus and their writings were kept thousands of years. Unlike the paper one would write on today, which wears away after a few years."

"And what do you write?"

"That is my secret," said Suliman.

"And how do you make papyrus?"

"Come, I'll show you."

To produce the rolls of papyrus, Suliman would cut long stalks of Cyperus, remove the bark, and cut the hollow reed into thin strips of about fifteen inches long, which he would then fasten to each other. For the first layer, he interwove a thin layer of stalks, fastened them together and placed another layer crossing in the opposite direction. Using a round, hewn stone, he tightened and polished the Cyperus stalks as Dudi's admiring eyes saw them turn into papyrus scroll.

For writing, Suliman used a long quill. He dipped it in black ink produced from a shellfish that lives on the shores of the lake, and with it he drew various letters and landscape paintings of the lake and its surroundings, much to Dudi's amazement. The hours passed, flocks of birds circled the sky and sought refuge from the predators of the night as the lake changed its colors in preparation for sunset.

"They'll be worrying about you back home," Suliman said. "I know you have two questions to ask me. I will give you the answers on another occasion."

How did he know I had two questions? Dudi pondered as he walked with excitement back to the village.

The next day, in the hot hours of the afternoon. Dudi rushed to the mud village.

After sipping the sweet tea Suliman had served him, his host said, "The first question you wanted to ask me was where my Hebrew is from? And the answer is simple. My grandfather was the head of the village who was transferred with all the villagers from the Damascene hills to the swamps. Before he passed away, he made my father swear that I, his beloved grandson, would get an education. The only way my father could keep his vow was to send me to study at an evangelical boarding school in Nazareth. The prevailing language there was English, but learning Hebrew was mandatory.

"The answer to your second question: I made my acquaintance with the papyrus at that boarding school in Nazareth. There was a wonderful library where I came across hieroglyphics, and I was immediately captivated. As soon as I flipped through the book, I felt close to the script. The icons on the papyrus felt familiar to me and the five-thousand-year gap between me and the ancient Egyptians was simply erased.

"I would imagine them going down to the lake to chop Cyperus and write their words of wisdom on it. During my time at the boarding school, I met a history teacher, an old priest, who was happy to hear about my familiarity papyrus. At his request, I brought him a few reeds and he shared with me his interest in hieroglyphics and the papyrus on which they were written. For many months he taught me the methods of processing the papyrus. Everything I know is owed to him. Have I answered your two questions?" Suliman turned to Dudi. "Do you have any more?"

"Yes. How did you know what my two questions were?"

Suliman lay his smart eyes to him and said, "There are benefits to age and experience, one of which is the ability to read minds. So, for example, I know you have another question."

Dudi was amazed. "How do you know that?"

"The ability to read minds comes with the understanding of the mind. But the answer to your interest as to where I got my blue eyes from, will come at another time."

***

The boat was not in its usual spot, nevertheless, Dudi knew that the door was open to him at all hours. He entered the room and sat down in his usual chair at Suliman's. A blue light flooded the room, and when he lifted his head, he saw in the doorway a girl dressed in a white galabia, her skin brown and radiant, her hair black and wavy, and eyes bluer than any he had ever seen. Bluer than the spring sky, and the water of the lake at sunset.

"My grandfather asked me to let you know he was on his way." She smiled at him with white teeth like a string of pearls and narrowed her eyes to two, tight blue slits. "I know your name is Dudi. Grandpa told me about you."

Before Dudi could get ahold of himself, Suliman appeared. His eyes, filled with both wisdom and sensitivity, immediately read Dudi's mortification and his granddaughter's joy.

"This is my granddaughter Tamara," he said as he hugged her.

Dudi was bewildered. The old man with the white hair plowed with wrinkles and bent by the years stood embraced with an upright and smiling mysterious flower, both boasting the same twinkling blue.

Too bad my mother is not here, he suddenly thought. She is always proud of the blue mimosa that blooms in our garden... she would never believe that there are bluer things in this world.

"Have a seat and I'll tell you the story," Suliman offered. "And in the meantime, our blue mimosa will serve us tea."

That is it! Dudi marveled. Where did the mimosa come from?!

Suliman burst out with a thunderous laugh and revealed his perfect teeth that withstood the effects of time.

"I promised you the story," he said. "It goes well with the Caucasian tea that Tamara is pouring for us."

"In the high Caucasus mountains there was a village called Chukilo," he began. "I know you haven't heard of it, but it's okay, no one has. In the village lived a happy family, 'Chukilo' was the name. Yes, you guessed it, the village was named after the family because they were the only ones there. The family would earn their keep raising sheep and by producing white wines unrivaled by any vineyard throughout the Caucasus as well as some field crops. On summer nights, the entire small tribe would gather in the large courtyard of the family winery, where they played bouzouk, blew kazoos and sang songs about war and love with words higher than the surrounding mountains.

"During winter, the snow would pile up to the windows and cut off the village from the rest of the world. Those were good times. Each family in its own home sitting around a pot in which they would make the national beverage of tea made from special bushes that grew in the local mountains. On those chilly days, they would warm their hearts in song and melody while sorting tea leaves and grains of rice.

"Everything was chopped in one swoop. The never-ending wars in the Caucasus also reached Chukilo, when a column of hungry, tired, and cruel troops conquered the village. They murdered most of the men and took the rest captive, raping the women, and looting anything they could find. After three days of killing, raping, and pillaging, the perpetrators left the village. Those who survived, physically and mentally wounded, left the destroyed village and set out on a long journey of hardship and torment, south to Turkey.

"After nine months of wandering, at the end of a large forest in central Turkey, my great-grandmother, who was fifteen years old, felt labor pains. She knew what to do and she went into the forest where she gave birth to a baby girl. Moments before she was about to strangle her, she pulled away and gazed at her. Something stopped her from disposing of the reminder of the horror of rape and the heavy load of memories. In our tribe, fifteen-year-old girls were experienced midwives. They would help their mothers and often their grandmothers give birth. With expert skill, the birthing mother cut the cord, wrapped the baby in her shirt, and went back to tell the mother about the birth. When the baby opened her eyes, she looked up at her mother with an astounding clear blue that captivated her heart and made her break down uncontrollably in tears of joy and relief.

"That's it, now both you and Tamara know the whole truth about where the blue eyes are from."

Dudi was thrilled. He thought he saw, or perhaps he was imagining, a blue tear fluttering in the corner of Suliman's eye, and a tear of the same color rolling down his granddaughter's cheek. The three could hear the silence descending upon the hut, with its own unique sound.

"Everything I told you and more about my family's wanderings through the prairies of Damascus and how it was moved by the Ottomans to the mud village, is written in my papyrus. So, now Dudi, you have your answer to the questions you wanted to ask about our blue eyes and about what I have been writing all this time."

***

Dudi would pay Suliman many visits. He loved to hear his fascinating stories, and enjoyed no less spending time with Suliman's granddaughter, who captured his heart.

Tamara adored her grandfather. Dudi's attentive listening to the stories seemed to have strengthened the bond between Tamara and her grandfather.

Grandpa needs an audience and now he has it, she thought to herself, smiling. She rediscovered her grandfather as one open and eager to tell his wonderful stories. Even the story of the origin of the blue eyes was new to her.

Dudi's visits to the hut became more frequent. He indeed came to hear Suliman's stories just as much as to spend many magical hours with his granddaughter. At one of their encounters, the two sat on the wooden bench Suliman had built and placed in the narrow gap between the lake shore and the mud house.

Tamara entered the hut and returned with a mosquito trap. She removed the dead mosquitoes with a dry bundle of herbs and applied a new batch of carob honey to the bowl.

"You know," she said with dreamy eyes. "I want to be a doctor."

"Why a doctor?" Dudi asked, surprised.

"When I was studying at the Anglican School in Nazareth, we spent four hours each week volunteering.

I served at the Scottish Hospital in the city, where I saw the fever and the many victims who got it and eventually died."

Once again, Tamara entered the hut to place the bowl down, and when she returned, she stood in front of him at her full height and asked, "What do you want to be when you grow up?"

"I am going to be a writer," he replied to her without any sign of bashfulness.

"Can anyone be a writer?" she asked, astonished.

"Yes," he replied. "Provided you have flowing hands, a good story, and a lot of imagination."

"I suppose you know your own writing skills well," she said affectionately. "But what story do you have to tell?"

"I have lots of stories, but the first one I write will be based on your grandfather's stories, they are so fascinating."

"And what about imagination?" she asked, arching her body.

"I envision plots about a beautiful girl who led her family from the distant Caucasus mountains to a remote village on the shores of a small lake and the story of her love for a young man from a nearby village..."

"Yes, you have a lot of imagination..." she replied with flushed cheeks.

The next day, Dudi appeared and handed Tamara a rolled papyrus.

"What's is?" she asked.

"Until I write my first book. I got this papyrus sheet from your grandfather yesterday and wrote a short children's story. I dedicate it to you."

Tamara opened the papyrus curiously and read it out loud:

"A Lake Wedding

All the animals in the lake came to the wedding. Fish, birds, various diggers, foxes, jackals, and the guest of honor – a gray wolf who came especially from up the Golan Heights.

The groom, a vibrant Kingfisher, brushed his feathers and stood on a branch kissing the water, looking lovingly at his bride, a gray catfish who pulled her head out of the water and wiggled her mustache with excitement.

Four nutrias stood in four corners, each holding a long reed holding a canopy of Cyperus inflorescence. The Swamp Cats Band entertained the guests. Two yellow-eyed cats howled a duet of love songs, and six pelicans rattled background melodies in their broad beaks.

A stork carrying a cane circled in the sky hinting heavily to the young couple. The guest of honor from the Golan Heights, stood on the edge of the water, ready to begin the ceremony.

"Repeat after me," he addressed the eager groom. "Will you marry me, in sickness and in poor, happily ever after?"

The colorful groom repeated after the wolf.

"I do! I do! I do!" the catfish replied with her mouth open, and her eyes veiled to the cheers of the crowd.

"Now, give her the ring," the wolf instructed the kingfisher and handed gave him a shiny acorn.

The kingfisher grabbed the wedding ring with his beak, looked at the catfish with piercing eyes when suddenly, he forgot his role and the celebratory status, dropped the acorn, dived into the water, grabbed the catfish with his beak and swallowed her in the blink of an eye to the sound of the crying guests.

Walking up the path to the Golan, with droopy ears and his tail between his back legs, the wolf growled to himself, "I knew they were wrong for each other from the start."

Tamara's jaw dropped before she burst out in sudden laughter. "I believed you had a rich imagination," she exclaimed. "But not that rich!"

She kept the papyrus to herself and sent Dudi on his way.

Thoughts of her laughter stayed with him in each step back to his village.

***

The night was dark. Dudi lay in his bed with open eyes, listening to the sounds of the night. He heard the owl that lived in a wedge between the rood slates serenading his hen as well as to other birds of the night that led their flocks shrieking to prey that they found dead in a field.

A cow bellowed in her sleep, and a hungry kid was looking for his mother goat. When the rooster crowed, he knew that in one more hour the sun would rise over the Golan Heights. He went out into the yard with sleep in his eyes and met his mother making her cheeses.

"Why did you wake up so early?" she said half-asking half-stating.

"I have plans," he told her.

After seeing Ali open the barn gate and leading the cows to the green pasture, Dudi turned to the lake. The sun rose and with it came the heat. He went straight to Suliman's house. The grandfather was not at home, but those stunning blue eyes were waiting for him.

"Come," Tamara told him. "Grandpa gave me the boat for the day."

Part of the boat was out of the water, and its bow was tied with a rope to a wooden post.

"Sometimes..." Dudi recalled the grandfather's words. "Sudden winds from the east turn the tranquil lake into a tumultuous and dangerous place. That is why I always tie the boat and keep a part of it out of the water."

Tamara untied the knot, walked into the water barefoot and pulled the boat in.

"Take your shoes off." She chuckled. "Nobody will steal them from here."

Slightly embarrassed, Dudi silently took his shoes off and got in the boat.

The boat was concave and flat, suited for the shallow lake. Tamara held the two oars with great skill and began rowing further onto the lake. The view was spectacular. From the center of the lake, one could see in all four directions of the sky: the green mountains of the Golan Heights and the Galilee to the east and west, the white Hermon to the north, and the basalt rocks to the south. The whole lake was fenced in with reeds and Cyperus and resembled a pearl embraced by the love of an oyster.

The lake was buzzing with life. Flocks of fearless coots cleared the way for the boat. White cranes stood on tree branches, indifferent to the boat cruising by them. Large catfish swam near the boat, alongside tilapia fish, who kept a distance from the pelicans and cormorants seeking the taste of a nice fat fish.

At the not-too-distant shore a pair of otters continued their tedious work digging tunnels and building dams, and a yellow swamp cat sunbathed, cuddling the crowded reeds while his eyes reflected the color waterlilies near him. The boat cruised along the shore, passing plane trees, white willows, and poplars.

"Wopal!" Dudi called to Tamara when he saw on the beach to his left his own personal oak tree.

The two pulled the bow of the boat to shore and sat down on the tree trunk, awkward and silent.

"You managed to put me to shame." Tamara broke the silence. "I thought I knew every corner of the lake. This really is a wonderful spot."

A flock of pelicans raised their noisy wings right in front of their eyes and saved Dudi from more awkwardness.

"This will be our spot," he replied with exhilaration.

The blue eyes met the brown ones with a warm, caressing gaze, and then it happened. Tamara placed her palm on his left palm.

"According to legend," Dudi said unsettled. "Love is in the heart, but for me it is in the palm of my left hand." His hand trembled with excitement and his fingers hugged hers.

Her fingers responded to his, and so their fingers twisted in a love dance.

After an eternity of silence, with their fingers crossing, the two brought their lips together for a kiss. Hours went by and the sun was about to set.

Tamara got in the boat. The white galabia she always wore stretched over her body, accentuating its curves.

"We'll meet here tomorrow," she said and pushed the boat into the water and navigated it south to the mud village with her back to Dudi.

He remained seated and watched the boat drift away as he drowned in the intoxicating landscape telling himself, this must be what heaven is like.

***

The lake water moistened the trunk of the oak tree. Dudi sat on his regular perch – a thick root that came out of the bottom of the trunk and formed a kind of step. It was the afternoon. A westerly sun washed the lake golden, and a light breeze created soft ripples on the surface of the water. Dudi was there early as he was struck with uncontainable anticipation.

The boat emerged quietly and, on its bow, sat Tamara in her white galabia. Her black locks draped over her shoulders, her lips were parted, and her eyes sent him a message of longing. The boat touched the shore and not a word was said. Suddenly, Tamara lifted her galabia over her head, exposing her naked body.

Dudi was stunned. The only female he had ever seen naked was his mother. It happened one time when she was showering in the yard and had asked him to bring her the bucket of water she had set for heating the stove indoors. He placed the bucket by the shower door, and for a split second saw her naked. The awkward moment was erased at dinner with a small smile between two people sharing a secret.

Now, Dudi was looking at Tamara's body, her small copper-colored breasts and charcoal nipples, her long bare legs, and her enticing flat belly. The seconds seemed like an eternity to Dudi. He soaked in the wonders of her body and prayed that the sight would never end.

Tamara dropped the galabia to the ground and stared right into his eyes.

He reached his arms toward her, and she said, "I have to go back. Grandpa needs the boat. See you tomorrow." The boat turned around, leaving Dudi alone with his needs and yearnings.

A muffled growl awoke Dudi from slumber. A grumbling noise came from the Golan Heights. When he went out, he saw his mother rushing to pick up the dishes from the barn in the yard.

"Go to the barn and make sure that everything is closed," she ordered. "An autumn storm is coming, and the cows will not graze today."

The storm rolled down the mountains and into the lake. Fierce winds raised high waves and turned the calm lake into a stormy sea. The experienced reeds let the storm pass over their heads. The winged creatures disappeared, the fish dug themselves into the shallow bottom, heavy rain misted the lake and its surroundings. Hours later, the storm ceased with the same suddenness with which it had begun, leaving behind tranquil waters as if nothing happened.

The crown of reeds that surrounded the lake rose lazily as the mud that swirled in the storm slowly set. The winged beasts filled the sky once again, knowing that the end of the storm provided an opportunity. A flock of petrels joined the seekers of the plethora of fish, crabs, and snails that the storm had brought to the surface of the water. Water turtles, nutrias, and wild cats immerged from their burrows to hunt and bask in the sun that had come out of hiding.

In the afternoon, after the rain had stopped, Dudi went down to the mud village. The dirt road was slippery and covered with branches and leaves. He entered the village on his way to Suliman's house and he almost stopped breathing. By the house he saw dozens of people, their feet immersed in the lake, holding long poles, looking for something in the murky water.

Suliman stood next to his house with a frozen expression and eyes almost shut.

"Tamara took the boat and disappeared," he said when he recognized Dudi.

Dudi's heart felt like it was pinched by a pair of tongs. He knew where to look for her. Without a single word he turned back and ran up the pigs' trail to the oak tree. Only feet from the shore he saw the boat turned upside down. He turned the boat over and found Tamara lying on her back. The galabia she wore was drenched in mud, but her beautiful face was clean, and her blue eyes were open. Her eyes seemed surprised yet peaceful.

Dudi lifted Tamara in his arms and stumbled to his perch on the big trunk. In the distance he saw the villagers approaching holding their long sticks. He kissed her eyes shut, keeping her blue gaze to himself, knowing that his life would never be the same again.

Suliman picked up her body, keeping his face strong like an iron mask. He stared at her for a while, and with a great deal of pain, turned his head to Dudi and said, "Everything is from Allah."

After that, he boarded his boat with her body and sailed toward the village. The others walked behind in the water in a mourning march, still holding their sticks.

The next morning Dudi returned to the tree trunk staring at the water that had returned to its original color. Before his eyes he saw a precession of boats carrying people in white grieving garments sailing north, to the village cemetery at the foot of the Golan Heights. He shuddered as he dreaded coming to terms with the death of a pure and beautiful soul.

Doubt and pain scorched his soul. I do not want to be there, he told himself, sitting for long hours on his tree trunk.

In the evening he saw the convoy of boats returning to the mud village. One of the boats veered in his direction. When he got to Dudi's perch, the bent and broken grandfather took out a long leather scroll from the hem of his robe and handed it to Dudi, only to continue his journey without uttering a word.

With trembling hands Dudi opened the cylinder and pulled out a papyrus soaked in his beloved's delicate scent. On the papyrus he saw the story he wrote and around it, wonderful illustrations of all the animals mentioned in the story. On the margins of the papyrus was written in small gold letters: "With great love."

Dudi hugged the papyrus that tore his heart and cried out from the depths of his soul, "There is no god!" He wandered home in the dark.

CHAPTER 3 – THE UNDERGROUND

The drum beat echoed at the entrance to the village, calling upon all to gather around the main square. The drum was placed on a cart pulled by two mules and a heavy-set Turkish drummer, dressed in a tattered military uniform, striking with all his might as if his life depended on the intensity of each blow.

Riding behind him on a black mare was an officer wearing a peaked cap, a red army coat adorned with gold fringes on his shoulders, and a long sword strapped to his chest. Further behind him, ten mounted troops trotted behind him in their frayed military uniforms.

"What is it this time?" the worried villagers muttered among themselves on their way to the square. They knew it could not be anything good if the Turks had something to do with it.

The caravan stopped as they reached the paved square. The officer motioned for one of the riders to approach and handed him a cardboard roll.

The rider took out a sheet of paper from the roll and read out in broken Hebrew, "The great sultan hereby informs his subjects of their obligation to surrender half of all their khubz to fund the war against the infidels.

Whoever fails to do so, shall meet the noose in the center of Damascus."

The drummer resumed his beat and the small caravan turned around and left the village. The villagers were in shock. The economic situation throughout the land, the plagues, and the "bakshish" that lined the pockets of Turkish officials drained their blood, and now came yet another decree. Each turned back home with their heads bowed in grief.

The Jewish residents of the land of Israel experienced the decline of the Ottoman Empire firsthand. For four hundred years, the empire ruled the Middle East and the land of Israel since it was first conquered by Sultan Selim I in 1516. Its fall was expedited in the summer of 1914, with the outbreak of The Great War.

England, France, and other countries set off to defend the Suez Canal, which the empire relied on as a major international trade route. England decided it needed to push the Ottomans east and north. For three years England and its allies fought the obstinate Turks, losing approximately six thousand soldiers in the ongoing bloody campaign. The Turkish army suffered similar losses.

As part of their war effort in the region, the British mobilized their Imperial Camel Corps Brigade and reinforcements of Australian troops that included among many, a mounted division.

The Turks, on the other hand, bolstered their forces with five German squadrons led by a company of balloons. It was in this war that the English army developed the theory of intelligence, involving the preventive intelligence system, which included a network of agents and spies in various countries around the world. A particular deception maneuver used to conquer Beersheba is still taught in military schools today.

To block the British advancement from northern Egypt, the Turks built a line of defense that stretched between Gaza and Beersheba. The British tried several times to breach that line but to no avail, leading to thousands of casualties on both sides during these attempts. The creative solution to this gruesome situation came from the rising star of the British Army, intelligence officer Edmund Allenby.

One sizzling summer day Turkish soldiers noticed two English cavalry riding toward them from the south. The Turks sent forces to capture them, yet they managed to escape but not before they dropped a large leather bag containing many documents. The bag was handed over to Turkish intelligence, who pounced on the loot like a hungry eagle on a carcass of a cow.

The Turks realized they were holding in their very hands the British Army's plan of their assault on Gaza. These documents included detailed plans, order of battle, unit numbers, names of commanders, detailed logistical needs, the number of horses prepared for battle and even their pedigree.

The material was taken for quick examination by the Turkish Intelligence Research Unit in Gaza, who confirmed that the documents were authentic and dependable. Soon after receiving this confirmation, the Turkish commander ordered the reinforcement of Gaza's line of defense. For this, Turkish units in the area were diluted, including those camped in the city of Beersheba.

Concurrently, General Allenby led a special task force that left the Sinai Peninsula and flanked Beersheba from the east. The few Turkish soldiers left in Beersheba were surprised by the attack, and the city fell to the English almost without a fight.

The economic distress in which the Ottoman rule found itself as a result of its wars led Turkish governors to treat subjects throughout the empire, including the Jews who lived in the Land of Israel, with a heavy hand. Almost every day, they would be plagued by decrees that made their lives unbearable. They set their hopes to the south, to the British Army. Beyond hope, various groups and organizations formed throughout the Land of Israel, who secretly helped the English and awaited the removal of the Ottoman rule for good.

***

"When are we going to start moving? This nonsense has been going on for two hours now!" Zelda, one of the ladies sitting in the carriage complained.

"We are waiting for one more passenger to join us," Gershon the coachman replied.

"The Messiah will arrive before that happens," complained Moishe, who was worried he would be late for his meeting in Safed.

"Great, let him come, pay two Bishliks, and we'll finally be on our way," said the coachman.

"I just think back for a second of when you took us about a month ago and asked us to get off the carriage near Safed and help you push it with the horse, and already my back is aching," Zelda added.

The Messiah never came, but Mendel, the eighth passenger showed up, paid his two Bishliks and Gershon motioned to the horses to get moving.

The Diligence was a carriage pulled by two horses, consisted of two wooden benches meant for eight passengers. The carriage was part of the transportation services operated by Kurtzman from Rosh Pina.

Kurtzman was a local tycoon. He owned a massive estate in the center of Rosh Pina, which boasted a large house surrounded by a broad yard that would serve as a parking lot for the Diligence carriages as well as freight wagons.

A Diligence would go from Rosh Pina to Safed five times a week. Once a week to Tiberius and another to Metula. The road to Safed traversed up the mountain and passengers would often be asked to step off the carriage and walk beside it to alleviate some of the weight the tired horses had to pull. Now and then, on snowy days in the Safed mountains, passengers would push the carriage up the snowy road.

The carriages were operated by hired coachmen. The front was for passengers, and the back had room for luggage and other belongings. A suitcase weighing up to one rotel[2] would be allowed aboard the carriage for free, however, heavier suitcases were charged according to the length of the trip. The carriages would leave on set days, yet the time of departure was quite flexible. A Diligence stagecoach would leave only once passengers had filled all the seats.

The horses were the kings of the stagecoaches, but the dirty transport work was left for the mules. The mule, a tough animal with great endurance, was used to transport cargo on roads or weights that were not suitable for the elegant horses. However, attempts to use the mules to transport the stagecoaches failed. Afterall, there is a reason for the

2. **Rotel** is a Turkish weight measurement equivalent to one pound.

saying "stubborn as a mule." Time and again, a mule would decide to stop halfway up the road and there was no forcing it to move, not even the anguish of a woman in labor, or the pleas of a farmer, who saw his planned meeting with a merchant in Haifa go down the drain.

Passengers who wanted to get to Haifa or Jerusalem traveled in Kurtzman's carriages to Tiberias, where they would switch carriages. In exceptional cases, there was an option to book a special trip from Rosh Pina to Haifa, which lasted about six consecutive hours.

The stable that stood at the end of the lot was intended for the care and feeding of the animals that served the transport network. The horses earned the central part of the stable, while the mules were housed in the fringes. The stone house in the center of the estate was two stories high.

In one part of the first floor lived Kurtzman's family, while in the other part there was a soup kitchen, where his wife, Chava, would serve home-cooked food for passersby, coachmen, and simply hungry people. The second floor that had a separate staircase, served as a hostel, and offered four beds in each room.

The stone house also served as the area's main post office. Letters and other postal items sent by residents of Rosh Pina, Yesodot, and other communities went through the post office. After sorting, the items were transported by carriages to Safed, Jaffa, and Jerusalem for distribution.

Postal items destined for abroad would have been transported to Jaffa and from there by ships around the world.

Kurtzman also provided residents with express mail services at a price of ten Bishliks per action. The express mail was sent by a horseman, who would ride for about seven hours from Rosh Pina to Haifa, and from there the mail was transferred to another horseman, who galloped the additional five hours to Jaffa.

In addition, Kurtzman's estate also served as a veteran "parliament." Every Friday, Rosh Pina veterans gathered in the courtyard joined by veterans from other communities. One could often meet guests from Safed and even faraway Metula, who would all gather with friends to talk at length about current affairs. In these meetings chaired by Kurtzman, participants often shared their problems, mostly revolving around the Turkish army and its actions. Nevertheless, Kurtzman was not only an entrepreneur and a shrewd businessman, but he also had other interests.

One day, Dudi arrived at the transportation hub, shortly before a loaded freight wagon hitched to a mule was about to leave for Safed. He paid the coachman one Bishlik and instructed him to deliver the packed cheeses to Rosenfeld's in Safed. Once the carriage left, Dudi walked into Kurtzman's office in the big house.

"Suliman told me you wanted to talk to me," he said to Kurtzman.

As far as Dudi was concerned, Suliman had always been a mysterious man of many faces and connections.

"Right," Kurtzman replied. "Suliman is a good friend, and he speaks highly about you. Besides, I see you use our services quite often."

"Yes," Dudi replied. "I sell my mother's cheeses in Safed and Haifa."

"Nice," the great Kurtzman said. "Perhaps you could be useful to us."

"I'd be happy to," Dudi replied, proud for being approached in that manner. "How can I help?"

"On your next trip to Safed, come by my way."

Days later, Dudi showed up at Kurtzman's office.

"I would like to ask you to deliver this envelope to my man at the Safed station. This is a personal letter," he told him.

"With pleasure," Dudi replied, taking the envelope. At the touch of his fingers, he noticed that the envelope was empty. When he tried to pay for the trip, the coachman informed him that he had been instructed not to charge him a fee.

At the station in Safed, he got out of the carriage and rushed to the station manager, who was waiting outside the office, and handed him the letter.

The manager took the envelope with a crooked face and quickly hid it in his pocket. Without saying a word, he sent him on his way.

A few days later, Dudi showed up at Kurtzman's office again and said, "I'm going again to Safed today."

"Good," Kurtzman replied. "But when I give you a personal letter, you should not pull it out in front of everyone. I could have easily sent a coachman to do that."

Dudi nodded solemnly.

Then, and after a brief angry pause Kurtzman said, "I have another letter to send."

Dudi received another sealed envelope and hid it in his pocket. Once again, he was convinced that the envelope was empty.

In Safed, he waited until all the passengers got off the carriage and for the coachmen to lead it to the parking lot before he would follow the manager to the office. Then, once he made sure that there was no one around he handed him the envelope.

The next time he met Kurtzman, Dudi advised that this time his trip would be longer as he was going to Haifa.

"Excellent," Kurtzman replied. "I have another personal matter. Please take the envelope from my man in Safed and deliver it to the manager of the station in Haifa. He will be waiting for you."

Dudi got in the carriage without having to pay for the ride. In Safed, while changing the carriages, he went into the office, received an envelope and in the blink of an eye hid it away in his pocket. This envelope was also empty.

During the rest stop, on the way to Haifa, his curiosity got the best of him, and when no one was looking, he took the envelope out and held it up toward the sun. As he suspected, it was empty.

In Haifa, he unloaded the cheese, waited for the local manager to finish dealing with the carriage before he would enter his office. Following the precautionary rules, he took out the envelope and swiftly handed it to the manager, who hurried to hide it in the bottom drawer.

Dudi said goodbye to the manager with a smile. It was already late, and he had no choice but to stay in a modest room at the nearby Anglican Hostel.

After several more similar transactions, Dudi re-entered Kurtzman's office.

"Do you have any other empty letters for me to forward?" he asked him insolently.

Kurtzman burst out in laughter. He obviously liked the tall, cheeky young man.

"Come with me," he said and led him to a tiny room behind his large office. "I know you understand that there is nothing in the letters, but I had to test you. So are the rules. I trust you completely and want to tell you that I am part of a group whose purpose is to expel the Turks from the country. We need people like you."

Dudi was not surprised. "How can I help?" he asked so naturally, as if he was asking his mother what was for dinner.

"I've had my eye on you for a long time now," Kurtzman said. "You are a brave and smart guy and I'm confident in your loyalty to your family and your people. And what's no less important is that your job is advantageous as it allows you to move from one place to another without arousing suspicion."

Everything to do with the expulsion of the Turks was good in Dudi's eyes. Most people hoped for the English to come out victorious and banish the Turks from their land. He rose from his chair and proudly shook Kurtzman's lumbering, big hand.

"But I must warn you," he said before Dudi left. "This is dangerous. The Turks are vicious and hang anyone caught in espionage of any sort."

***

"I have a task for you," Kurtzman said, inviting Dudi to the tiny side room.

Dudi's ears perked up.

"Go to Acre, near the ancient port you will find the famous fish shop, Abu Salah. Ali Marwan's small cheese shop is right next it. He heard about "Hannah's Cheeses" and is interested in buying cheese from you. On the way back you will pass through Napoleon Hill. You cannot miss it – it is as tall as anything Napoleon had ever built. The Turkish cavalry battalion set up camp there some days ago. Our people want to know how many horses are in that battalion. I wish you success. By the way, I have something for you to give Marwan."

Dudi got on the stagecoach from Rosh Pina to Haifa. He got off at the sea junction and walked toward Acre. He entered through one of the gates of the outer city wall, right into the middle of market day.

Hundreds of stalls with a variety of products and colors spread out along the street, and vendors competed with their loud voices over the hearts of the diverse customers. In the whirlpool of buyers were farmers who came from nearby and distant villages and bargained with the hawkers for better deals; bundles of sage leaves for an old black angel rope, and a pile of herbs for a used keffiyeh.

Effendi walked around with curled mustaches looking for interesting finds like inlaid hookah from Istanbul, and maybe a string of precious stones from Mashhad in Persia as a gift for the woman they would leave at home. Jews in ultra-Orthodox dress mingled with Circassians in high-brimmed hats, Druze wearing white crowded next to priests in black clerical uniform, and groups of adventure-seeking children running in between them all stirring up the commotion even more.

Dudi was surprised by the ruckus, which was in stark contrast to the serene village. He loved the noise and blended in with the crowd. As he worked his way down the market, the number of fish shops rose compared to the haberdasheries. The market was chopped at the port. He stood there, enthralled. The charming, ancient, and beautiful fishing port of Acre unfolded before him. Fishing boats anchored at the docks, and others sailed the sea, waiting their turn to get into the packed harbor.

Beyond the platform was a paved stone promenade and near it, crowded residential and commercial buildings, mosques, churches, and mansions – one of which was three stories high. Dozens of stores offered the finest goods in the country and even the world. Dudi walked dizzy between the minarets of the mosques, church domes, and the ornate arches of the opulent homes. A robust orchestra of Crusader and Muslim architecture.

His curiosity and enthusiasm were bubbling, but he knew that there was a task at hand. He found Abu Salah's large store with ease at the center of the platform. At the front of it, he noticed crates which the fishermen emptied fluttering fish into. The fish shop shared a wall with a tiny, obscured shop, Marwan's cheese shop. It had its own aroma, though it could not compete with those rising from Abu Salah's.

Marwan was not surprised by the visit. Dudi placed the package of cheese on the table and underneath it, hid the letter he had received from Kurtzman.

With a swift movement, Marwan pulled out the letter and hid it in the loose galabia he was wearing. He immediately pulled out from under the cheese table a set of scales, piling the cheeses on one side and the weights on the other.

"One and a half rotel," he said to Dudi, handing him a bundle of Bishliks. "Go in peace."

Dudi was happy to walk around the harbor and see the fishermen pulling the fish from the net, but true to his mission, he left town and headed toward Napoleon Hill. At the foot of the hill, he saw a group of hikers accompanied by a guide climbing the western slope. He joined the group and climbed up with them. The view from the top of the hill was exhilarating. The entire harbor looked like an innocent painting filled with sails and striking blue. Around the port, one could see the city's buildings, towers, and minarets encircled by the ancient wall.

After catching their breath from the tedious climb, the group stood up to look at the view, and the guide, with hands in his pockets and a hint of condescension of one who was about to ask a question only he knew the answer to, asked, "What is special about the hill we are standing on?"

And after ruling out a number of answers, he told the travelers, "They say that Napoleon was not only a brave commander but also a wise man. When he saw the remarkable walls of Acre, he realized he would not be able to take the city without reliable intelligence. To advance the attack, he decided to build a hill where he would be able to observe the city and the Turkish defense system. He issued an order that every soldier in his army must fill a bucket and stack the dirt into one pile.

"That dirt from the buckets created this hill you are standing on, which was later named 'Napoleon Hill.' And if we go back to my question as to what makes the hill so special, the answer is that it is higher than the walls and overlooks the Turkish fortifications as well as the entire city."

"So why are there double walls?" asked a curious traveler.

"Great question," the guide replied. "After Napoleon saw the walls, the guard towers, and the fortifications, he concluded that he could not breach the walls and decided to dig a tunnel underneath it to get into the city. He had underestimated the Turks. Once the tunnel was complete and Napoleon's soldiers tried to get into the city and the port, they discovered another wall that the Turks constructed swiftly, thus blocking their way into the city. At this point Napoleon despaired and ordered his men to retreat."

The guide's stories fascinated Dudi, but he was still very dedicated to his mission. He turned to the southern side of the hill, from which he saw Haifa Bay in all its glory – the city of Haifa at the southern tip to Acre in the north. However, at this point he was not there to enjoy the view. He turned to the northern part of the hill, and at its foot he found what he was looking for.

At the bottom of the hill, he saw a camp of tents built in a circle with a large pavilion in the middle. Next to it, was a plush carriage strapped to four white horses. In the plaza around the main pavilion, a group of Turkish soldiers were walking around, and another group was engaging in exercises. By the camp stood a pen with dozens of horses. A Turkish soldier appeared from one of the tents pushing a cart laden with hay, scattering it along the pen. The hungry horses lined up to eat, enabling Dudi to count them easily. When he had finished counting, Dudi went down the other side of the hill and hurried to the sea junction to catch the stagecoach on its way from Haifa to Rosh Pina. Despite the late hour, a light shined out of Kurtzman's office window.

Dudi knocked on the door and said, "Fifty-two and four more strapped to a carriage." And without waiting for a response, he waved goodbye and quickly set out to catch a ride back to the village.

This was Dudi's final test assignment. After that he was sent on additional intelligence missions, and made a name for himself as a trustworthy, brave man who could deliver the goods. The organization to which he belonged had dozens of members bound by trust and respect. In little time, he got to personally know most members and commanders.

The two commanders of the organization gained his admiration: Ami Ben-Ari and Yosef Menachemi. Ami was born in a village down south. When he was young boy, all had already agreed that he was meant for greatness. His prolific leadership had enchanted all around him and his dedication and belief in the need to expel the Turks from Palestine inspired many. It was no wonder he soon became one of the two commanders of the organization.

Yosef Menachemi was the opposite of his partner in command, and not just because he was born in the Galilee. He was introverted, considerate, sophisticated, humble, and known for his broad knowledge. An intelligent man in his soul. Rumor had it that General Allenby nominated him for the post of head of the Jewish state to be established in Palestine after the expulsion of the Turks.

***

Like a writer without words and a singer without song, frozen and at a loss, Dudi paused in front of his little house. Six sweaty horses stood at the entrance, roughly trampling his mother's vegetable garden, drinking water thirstily from bowls placed in front of them. On the path itself, six Turkish soldiers wearing grubby uniforms knelt to the east with their long-barreled rifles beside them.

It did not take much for Dudi to identify the commander. He was a massive man whose belly reminded him of one of the round Golan hills. The long mustache as that of the nutrias in the lake slumped and kissed his stomach.

When he entered his house, he saw his father sitting at the big table, his head buried in an old Mishnah book and his swaying body signaling severe distress. His mother sat on the other side of the table with her head resting between her trembling shoulders. His sister, Esther, lay on her stomach on the old sofa, and the pillow under her head was soaked with tears, spreading a salty scent of pain.

"What happened?" Dudi was horrified. "And what are the Turks doing outside?"

"They want to take Dad to Damascus for court martial and to tear down our house!" Hannah exclaimed and her cries turned into chopped sobs.

"Why?" Dudi was startled.

"They found the hideout!" his mother replied with what was left of her strength.

Silence wrapped the house. Not a sound was made. Until that moment, Dudi had no idea that disaster had a smell and a shape. His father's wabbly movements stopped and his head was buried in the Mishnah book on the table. His mother's body stopped shaking and her head sank into her shoulders until it was almost completely engulfed in them. His sister's long hair covered the wet pillow and her musky scent that he loved so much, travelled throughout the room. Dudi counted the silence. He felt like a black veil was covering his soul.

He suddenly found himself coming out of the silence through the kitchen's back door. He passed the barn and went down the path that led to the lake.

He met Suliman in his usual spot, which was exactly where he was when they had happily parted ways an hour before. The papyrus he was working on remained the same as well. Dudi sat down on the chair in front of him. Suliman did not utter a word and continued to peel off the reed. When he finally managed to collect his himself, he told Suliman, "The Turks want to court martial my father, tear down our house, and expel us from the village."

Suliman's sculpted copper face did not move, yet his wise eyes radiated empathy and distress.

"Why?" he asked.

"The Turks found the crops my mother hid. They want to punish us to teach everyone else a lesson."

"They are cruel people," Suliman replied. "You once asked me what else I write in my papyrus scrolls, and I didn't want to tell you. I write about that – their cruelty. They pray to Allah, but they are godless people. What are you thinking of doing?"

"I have made a decision, but I need your help," Dudi replied. He knew that Suliman had a connection with the Turks and so he leaned over to Suliman's ear and whispered something.

Suliman's stone face changed entirely.

"Are you sure?" he asked Dudi, studying his heart with his eyes.

"I have no choice. If not, the Turks will hang my father."

The next morning, the Turkish guard organized the demolition of the house and waited for the final approval from Abdul Bai, the high commander of the Sultan's army in the Galilee and the Bashan, however, approval was delayed.

Around noon, hoofbeats were heard in the distance. The rider got off his horse, tired and agitated, and turned to the commander of the guard, handing him a written letter.

The commander's chastened mustache changed direction and rose upward. His lips parted and his tongue protruded from his mouth. After reading the letter repeatedly, he turned to his soldiers and sounded a weak command, "We're leaving!"

The soldiers climbed on their horses and rode behind their commander on the road leading out of the village, toward Tiberias, the seat of the second cavalry brigade of the Sultan's army.

From that day, Dudi never saw Suliman and never set foot in the mud village again.

CHAPTER 4 – THE CONDEMNED

The courthouse in Damascus was in an old crusader building that would, from time to time, be amateurly reinforced so as to keep its walls from collapsing on its inhabitants. The hall itself was broad and its stone floor carried rows of dilapidated benches to seat the general public.

At the entrance, merchants would compete for the attention of the rank-and-file walking around aimlessly in the city square. No doubt, the favorite merchant of all was Ahmad, a tall, large man who would stand behind a wooden table covered in trays of Rahat Lokum.

Ahmad's Rahat Lokum was a popular dessert throughout Damascus. He would gladly share the recipe with anyone who would ask – gelatin, sugar, lemon juice, and corn flour. However, the spice mixture responsible for the unique flavors remained his well-kept secret.

"Everyone must have a secret to take with them to the grave," he would declare for the curious enquirers.

At the doorway to the courtroom stood two stern police officers watching the crowd and preventing the merchants from entering. The only merchant allowed in was an ostentatious fellow named Mustafa. He wore yellow trousers, a red top, and a blue silk Phrygian cap that had seen better days.

He inherited the license to sell Tamarind in the courtroom from his ancestors and was considered the number one expert in Damascus for brewing the miraculous drink.

Every evening Mustafa would prepare the sour-sweet drink for the next day using Tamarind acorns. Cuttings of the tree were brought hundreds of years ago from India and successfully propagated in various areas throughout the Middle East. He would soak the acorns at night in a metal container filled with water and then place it in the yard for the night chill to work its magic. In the morning he added the spices, and the drink was ready for the day. He would transfer the cool liquid into a beautiful, polished copper samovar, and head to work.

The samovar was bought by his grandfather's grandfather in the copper market in Kolkata, India. The copper vessel was adorned with mythological Indian figures. From its lower part came a twisting nozzle like that of milking a cow. At the end of the nozzle was a ceramic spout where the merchant would pour the brown drink into small cups.

Mustafa would rest the wide strap attached to the samovar around his neck and whenever it would empty, he would return to his house not too far from the square and refill it. The courthouse was his turf.

He would move swiftly between the benches and sell the drink in white ceramic mugs, adorned with traditional Armenian blue paintings. The mugs would be passed along from hand to mouth and from one mouth to the next in exchange for a few copper coins tossed into a leather pocket tied around his waist.

Every hour, he would approach the judge's bench to pour the drink into a special cup reserved only for him. According to the good old laws, the judge did not pay for the drink, and Mustafa did not have to pay for the license.

Only few courtroom visitors came for an actual reason. They sat in front of the courtroom, next to the judge's elevated bench. The majority of the audience was made up of people just walking by and professional idlers, who came to court to alleviate their day-to-day boredom.

The judge sat on a high chair that stood on a low raised platform overlooking the courtroom. He was wearing a shirt that was meant to be white, but someone must have forgotten the rules, and put over it a black robe adorned with gold stripes. He wore a cap he received many years ago from the secretary of the court upon his appointment as a regional court judge. An old fan swirled above his head, completing two spins per minute, and occasionally dispelling the heat and humidity that prevailed in the hall.

"Muhammad bin Ali," exclaimed the Shawish, who also served as the judge's personal assistant, both as the legal aid as well as clerk in charge of order and discipline in the courtroom.

Coming out of the nearby detention room, two husky police officers pushed in a frightened boy whose eyes rolled in their sockets like the wheels of a vending cart in the town square.

The judge held a sheet of paper he had pulled out of the pile that had covered the old table.

"You, Muhammad bin Ali, are accused of stealing the charity fund from the al-Qabria Mosque on Friday. Do you have anything to say in your defense?"

Shouts of contempt were thrown from the crowd at the boy, whose lips stayed closed and his chin pressed to his chest, remained silent.

"Does anyone want to say anything?" the judge said in a weary voice and turned to the crowd.

A man with a hunched spine advanced from the end of the hall. His hair draped down his face and over his long beard. A filthy white galabia wrapped his body down to the crumbling cloth sandals on his feet. He approached the Shawish, and with a trembling hand, offered him a white envelope.

The Shawish opened the envelope and began counting its contents. Seconds later, he shoved the envelope into a hidden pocket in the galabia he was wearing and blinked with his red eyes at the judge.

The judge winked at him with his left eye and announced while perusing the paper he was holding in his hand, "After reviewing the legal material and references shown to me by the Shawish, I rule to acquit the defendant and order his immediate release."

The two husky officers released the cuffs that bound the boy's wrists and ankles. The man in the striped galabia approached the boy and in a surprising motion that did not match his slender physique, slapped him across the face with such force that pushed the boy to the front door. The shocked audience enjoyed the free show, and even the Tamarind seller had stopped selling the drink for three long seconds.

"Silence in the court room!" shouted the Shawish. "We have a lot of work to do today!"

The crowd quietened down slowly.

"Fatima Bat Musa al-Karwani!" The judge announced the name of the next case and pulled out a sheet of paper from the pile. "You are accused of strangling your four-month-old son to death several months ago."

"What kind of mother kills her own baby?!" Protesting voices rose from the crowd, which was made up entirely of men.

Fatima seemed detached from her surroundings. Her eyes stared at the fan; her body tucked inside itself. She was absent-minded in the sweaty, hot hall occupied only by men.

"What is your answer?" the judge demanded.

Fatima did not notice at all that he had approached her, and she was muted with shock.

"Is there anyone present who would like to say something?" The judge hastily looked up from his papers, realizing that this case will not be as rewarding.

Several seconds later, he announced, "After reviewing the investigation material, and given that I did not receive any assistance from the audience, I sentence Fatima, daughter of Musa el-Karwani, to twenty-three years in prison."

And the guards rushed to get Fatima out of the courtroom.

The third case that morning was of Nahira. The judge declared, "She is charged with the murder of her husband!"

Shouts of contempt from the all-male audience were heard as she was forcibly seated on the accused's bench.

"Does anyone in the audience want to say something?" the judge asked without any expectations.

Before announcing the sentence, a small woman appeared from the end of the courtroom and shuffled up to the podium.

"Do you want to say something?" The judge turned to her indifferently.

"Yes," the old woman replied. "My daughter murdered her husband after he had thrown one of their children into a well."

"That is not an excuse," the judge replied to the cheering crowd. "A good Muslim woman must not harm her husband. For that she deserves the death penalty. Do you have anything else to say?" he asked in a hopeless voice.

The old woman slowly made her way to the Shawish and offered him a folded piece of newspaper with a shaking hand.

The Shawish turned his back on the crowd and faced the court, opened the folded newspaper and after a few seconds shook the left end of his mustache sloping toward the judge.

"That's not enough," the judge grumbled.

The Shawish mustache moved wearily. "Do not forget I have a wedding next week," he whispered to the judge.

The judge contemplated this information. There was no doubt that this was the most complicated case brought before him that day. After a few minutes he gave his verdict, "Given the special circumstances, I rule that the defendant must hand over her twelve children to an orphanage, and I forbid her from marrying until she dies."

Heavy booing came as a response to the verdict, haunting the judge who fled to his chamber, and Mustafa ran after him with the samovar to help his honor cool off with a glass of Tamarind.

The afternoon session was different. The court convened as a special state security court. The judge was the same judge, but next to him sat two military officers, who had replaced the officers' hats with red judges' turbans.

The courtroom was closed to the public, and a group of soldiers with long-barreled rifles in their hands encircled the building.

A company of Circassian riders were parked in the square to assist the soldiers if needed. Military officers in green uniforms occupied the benches.

The Shawish himself took advantage of the lunch break to change into the dilapidated work clothes he wore in the morning and returned to the courtroom in festive attire. Undoubtedly, something was going to happen.

The three judges sat tensed and perhaps the fan understood the gravity of the moment and had sped its pace up to three spins per minute. The only indifferent person was the man with the samovar. He continued to walk between the benches selling his drink for pennies to whoever needed their thirst quenched.

The courtroom was bubbling with excitement. The special military prosecutor stood beside the bench, staring intensely at the hallway that led from the detainees' cells in the courtroom dungeons.

The signal is given. Three large guards entered the courtroom and stood between the bench and the door from where the prisoners would enter. Two young prisoners were ushered into the courtroom. Their wrists and ankles shackled in heavy iron. Behind them stood another row of gruff guards.

The prisoners' faces were bruised. One face was swollen and completely obscured his left eye, the other prisoner's ears were almost torn from his head, and his lips were swollen and bleeding. The guards held them from all sides, to prevent them from collapsing.

The special military prosecutor cleared his throat, looked at the audience and then at the three distinguished judges. The courtroom was silent. Mustafa and the fan also stopped what they were doing. Aware of the gravity of the event, the military prosecutor read the indictment in an authoritative voice, "The Great Sultan and the Council of Sages hereby accuse Ami Ben-Ari and Yosef Menachemi, both from Palestine, of grave betrayal of the Turkish people and espionage in favor of the English infidels. Considering the severity of the charges, the prosecution requests they'd be sentenced to death."

***

The prosecutor lifted his head from the paper he was holding and with a great sense of purpose, glanced at the judges and the large audience that gathered in the room.

The judge addressed the prisoners and asked bluntly, "Do you have anything to say for yourselves?"

Shocked and battered and fearful, neither responded to the judge's question.

The head judge conferred with the other judges to his left and right and announced, "The court views the silence of the accused as a confession to all accounts. The court will adjourn for fifteen minutes."

The room was buzzing again. Mustafa announced his Tamarind juice, and the fan was back to three laps a minute. When the court reconvened, the Shawish called the audience to rise on their feet for the judges to walk in. Tension was at its peak.

The military prosecutor stared intently at the panel of judges. The head of the ensemble, aware of the gravity of the moment, perused the paper he was holding in his hands, raised his head and looked up proudly at the crowd.

"After examining all the evidence, and the circumstances, we sentence the defendants to death by hanging until their souls depart."

The Shawish called upon the crowd to stop their cries of joy but to no avail. The officers present roared in delight.

The gallows were raised hastily at "Marjeh Square," in the center of Damascus. The square was built near the old city by the Ottomans in the late 19th century as an execution spot, earning its nickname "Martyrs' Square." To be hanged in the square was an honor reserved to few. The average prisoners sentenced to death were strung up by the hundreds within prison walls throughout the city.

The Hanging Square was surrounded by shops, restaurants, guest houses, and hotels where rent included a premium for the free entertainment provided to their guests – an excellent view of the mass executions.

The gallows were composed of three wooden beams placed in the shape of a pyramid, about nine feet apart at their base, perched between the stones of the square and a vertex connected by strong sisal ropes. The pyramid rose to a height of thirteen feet, and a seven foot long rope would dangle from its center and at its end, a noose reinforced with twisting knots.

The mayor would sit on a tiny podium next to the gallows, and by his side, a brown-skinned Sudanese servant holding a parasol to protect the dignitary from the scorching sun. The mayor looked at the gallows and decided that the time had come for Damascus to also have elaborate gallows like those he saw in the main prison in Istanbul, with a trapdoor beneath the noose and upholstered chairs for dignitaries attending the ceremony.

Thousands of people crowded around the hanging facility waiting patiently and curiously for the week's main show. Entire families would come. Dedicated fathers placed their children on their shoulders, so they did not miss the show, and their wives, in colorful traditional clothing, found peepholes between the wall of men that surrounded the square. They did not want to miss the best show in town, which would provide them with much to talk about all week during their regular meetings by the well in the center of the perfume market.

On execution days, vendors would leave their regular posts at Damascus' famous market and head to Marjeh Square for a chance to increase their take. The food market that would appear by the square would sell the best Damascus would have to offer – lamb shawarma, Syrian hummus, hot peppers in brine, Syrian Falafel, Syrian style fava beans, and many such savory dishes alongside sweet stands selling, among many things, sugar coated fruit, various baklawa, and halva in one hundred assorted flavors.

A line of soldiers would separate the human circle from the two hanging gibbets, making sure to keep a wide and clear lane to the city's main street. Despite the long hours of waiting under the scorching Damascus sun, none of those present would think to give up the spot they had managed to claim by virtue of a long wait. And finally, the wait would pay off. The sound of drums would get closer.

A unit of twelve soldiers wearing tattered green uniforms that had not been washed since the last hanging on the last day of Eid el-Adha, marched on. An officer led the line while in the very back, horsemen in white clothes and orange turbans walked two mules adorned with flowers around their necks and wreaths to their ears. On the back of each sat a man in a white galabia, eyes covered with a piece of green cloth, hands tied behind their backs.

Cries of contempt erupted from the noisy crowd. Only the presence of the guards prevented spectators from lynching the prisoners. The horsemen led the mules to the center of the gallows. The commander placed the nooses around the necks of the prisoners and asked the mayor for approval to continue the ceremony. Once granted permission, two soldiers stood near the mules. An officer climbed a small ladder and removed the blindfolds. The two looked shocked and frightened by the roars of the eager crowd.

An old man came out of the crowd wearing a large black yarmulke, holding a prayer book. The rabbi approached the two prisoners, said a silent prayer, and hastily left the square as if his own life depended on it.

The two horsemen kicked the backsides of the mules with great force, making them rush away, leaving the convicts hanging to their deaths.

Fifteen minutes later, a military doctor called their time of death. The officer invited the mayor to attach a piece of cloth to the dangling bodies reading the words: "Thus shall be done to those who betray the sultan and the empire."

As the ceremony ended, while escaping the heavy heat and hunger that plagued him, the mayor decided that in the new gallows that he would build he will add an even more luxurious guest room than the one in Istanbul Central Prison, where he had been invited to back in the day to witness the hanging of seven Kurdish rebels.

***

Dudi sat in the hall of the arched building that was home to the Scottish hostel. From the arched door in the entrance, one could notice the hall's high ceiling, the coarse stone floor, and the raw wooden counter. The building served as a Turkish khan before it was purchased by the Scottish church. It offered twelve modest rooms for pilgrims on their way to Nazareth and Jerusalem. On a regular day, meaning most of the time, the lodge was empty and offered its services to whoever needed a cheap, clean place to sleep in downtown Haifa.

Such accommodations were quite scarce. All the beds tended to be in dodgy places. Some offered Dudi a bed in a room with other passing guests, who would spread pungent and unpleasant odors, while others offered unventilated rooms with floors that had not been washed for days, and whose occupants shared filthy toilets that only made him miss the outhouse back home in the village.

The Scottish hostel had two advantages. First, it was cheap – one Turkish Lira per night. Second, the hostel manager; a tall, large man who would introduce himself as Jerry. After placing his bag in the small, clean room, Dudi accepted Jerry's invitation to sip English Earl Gray tea with him in the hostel lobby. The cup of tea became a whole kettle, and Didi found himself fascinated by his host's stories, which extended into the night.

An instant connection was formed between the two, perhaps because of the arched space, perhaps the aroma of English tea, and perhaps Jerry's unique personality. He came across as a charming man who knows how to captivate his audience with sensitive and intimate closeness.

It was during that first meeting that Jerry said he was sent by the Scottish Church to run the place. "We have a tradition called 'Mission for the benefit of the Community,'" he said.

As part of this mission, he was sent to run the hostel that would serve the pilgrims who were members of the church, and at the end of his mission he would return to his life in parish near St Paul's Church in north London. He further said that due to the few pilgrims at this time of year as well as the meager income, he also works as the receptionist and does the maintenance.

Jerry finished sipping his tea, poured some more for Dudi, and went as usual to listen to the evening news on the BBC. When he returned, he turned distraught to Dudi, and said, "Did you hear what the Turks did?"

"What do you mean?" Dudi asked.

"I just heard that those bastards hanged two Jews who spied for England."

A huge lump of pain and despair choked Dudi's throat.

Jerry was so worried, he rushed to get him a glass of water.

Dudi took a seat on a wooden chair with his body shaking and his face white as a ghost.

"Should I call the doctor?" Jerry asked.

Dudi rejected his offer with a simple hand gesture. With heavy knees, he stumbled to his room. Darkness pained his soul. The night prolonged and dawn delayed rising. Even in his darkest hours, he never turned to God. Not since he recovered Tamara's body from under that damned boat. How could God do that to a pure soul who had yet the chance to sin, he asked himself day and night. This time, he knew that there was no one to hear his protest. He looked deep into the truth and himself.

Little before morning, he fell asleep for hours of distress. When he woke, Dudi walked out of his room and discovered a jug of water placed on his doorstep. The reception was empty. He sipped his water and went out into the alley. Feeling lost and forsaken, Dudi wandered downtown, between the old buildings and garbage dumps. His feet led him from one little alley to another, until he stood in front of a large cylindrical stone building with a sharp, high spire. The two wooden doors in front of him were spaced apart. A shiny copper plaque was attached to one of them, reading the words: "The Scottish Hospital, Established in 1889"

He turned to the other door that had a small wooden cross above it. He pushed the heavy door in and entered the church's arched stone-walled nave. The eastern wall featured a vivid mosaic depicting the life of Christ. Out of the western wall, broad windows offered a view onto a small courtyard. At the entrance of the church stood a raised platform covered in red carpeting and at its center, an alter wrapped in a green, fitted mat, and by it a wooden podium.

The person behind the podium was exceptionally impressive. He was a tall man wearing a white robe, a golden sash to match the miter on his head.

Despite sitting in the back row, the priest's face fascinated Dudi's. It was red with a pair of blue eyes in the center. A deep scar crossed his face from the tip of his lip to his left ear.

The vicar delivered an enthusiastic sermon to the audience that filled the church: one old woman at the end of the front row who may or may not had fallen asleep at some point.

When he noticed Dudi come in, he gestured with his little finger. A slender boy emerged from behind one of the arches and handed Dudi a glass of chilled water that quenched his thirst.

The old lady from the front row suddenly woke up and turned to the exit.

The vicar looked straight at Dudi as if he were a world in its entirety. Dudi moved to the second row and the vicar continued with his sermon and shared his feelings with the audience which consisted of Dudi alone.

"Happiness is at the far end of despair," he said.

The words carved into Dudi's heart and evoked a wave of excitement in him. The vicar finished his words and remained standing behind the pulpit, sharing glances with Dudi. After a few minutes of silence, the priest gestured to a confessional that stood not far from the altar.

Dudi sat on a high chair in the booth, beyond the grille he saw the vicar's blue eyes and the scar across his face.

"Can I help you, my son?" asked the priest.

The direct words shook Dudi. He stared into the vicar's eyes and felt himself come apart. He burst into tears of desperation, and uncontrollable whimpers. The vicar's eyes radiated serenity and sympathy and made him experience compassion. After a few minutes, without uttering a single word, Dudi got up, went out of the confessional and onto the street, cleansed and pure.

The next morning, he went to the church misty-eyed. The church was the same church, and the vicar the same vicar. At the end of the sermon, the three believers sitting on the benches left, and Dudi entered the confessional.

"I decided to convert to Christianity," he told the vicar.

"It's not an easy decision," the vicar said.

"I know," Dudi replied. "It's my only way to break free from the burden of pain and move on with my life."

"I understand," the vicar replied. "I, too, had a difficult life."

"I'm sure," Dudi replied. "But you made a change in yours."

For the first time Dudi saw the priest's eyes close and the scar soften.

"Come in a week's time," he said following a long silent pause.

Dudi did not need a week. He knew that the only way to go was not to try to run away but rather come to terms with a new life, cut off from all sides.

"The city is small, and the tongues are long," the vicar said in their next meeting. "I'll give you an address in London, they know about you. If you don't change your mind, go to them."

Dudi hopped on the carriage from Haifa to Beirut. In his hand he held a backpack with some clothes and a Bible. Deep in his shirt pocket, he kept the note the priest had given him with the address in London. The carriage stopped in the port of Beirut. Dudi got off and walked straight to the Thomas Cook travel agency. The money he had was enough for a one-way ticket.

The ship was to sail in a few hours from then. In the middle of the harbor Dudi found what he was looking for, a new post office whose red colors stood out against the gray surroundings. He went to a letter box in the center of the post office and in it dropped the most important letter he would ever write.

***

Dear Mother,

My hands are trembling, and a storm is brewing in my soul, though I am determined to explain the message I sent you about going to London and converting to Christianity.

I am aware that knowing this must be tearing your soul apart and crushing your heart, but trust me, beloved Mother, I do not want to give you the details of what would be my other choice. I know how great your love is for me and pray, no matter to which god, that you will always keep a hint of love for me in your heart.

I did not come to this decision rashly but rather after long, tormenting days of anxiety and contemplation that peaked in two incidents of love and betrayal. I could share the love story with you but never did out of my adolescent pride or perhaps fearing your response and for that, I am deeply sorry.

I have experienced a great love, Mother, with such intensity I never knew I had within me. However, one strong wind from the east turned a boat over in the lake and drowned my love. The very next day, I went to the oak tree, feet away from where she had drowned and sat on the tree stump that my beloved and I shared. The lake was tranquil, the kingfisher was perched in his usual spot, and the Cyperus flowers were basking in the sun as if nothing happened.

Before me appeared the grandfather of Tamara, yes that was her name, a noble and wise man with his feet deep in the water, holding the body of his granddaughter, mumbling to himself or perhaps to me or to his god, "Kulu min Allah," everything is from God. That was the grandfather making his peace with his god. But what about ours? "The Lord has given, and the Lord has taken away; blessed be the name of the Lord." It was as if lightning had struck me. That is our peace with God? Just like that "The Lord has taken away?" And who? And why?

You did not know her, dear Mother. She was a wonderful friend. A child of nature with a soul bigger than the lake itself, filled with joy and laughter, and I loved her like the fish loves the water and like the flower loves spring, yet God took her away.

And for that we must bless the name of the Lord?

My eyes teared, my heart ached, and I screamed to the heavens alas, I received no answers or any sighs. Silence fell across the land and my faith broke.

As for the story of betrayal, I could not tell you at the time, but I have decided to now share my darkest secret with the only person in the world who might just understand me.

Surely you would remember the day those damned Turks came. We sat in our home surrounded by Turkish soldiers and waited for the next day when we would have to take Dad to court martial in Damascus. We knew that such a sentence would only end in a hanging. We also knew well that it was not only Dad's fate that had been doomed, but ours as well. By order of the Sultan, the soldiers had to destroy our house and our lives.

Dad's fate was in my hands. I slipped out of the house and went down to the mud village, the place you had warned me about my entire childhood. There, I met Suliman, Tamara's grandfather. I knew he had the connections we would need. I sent him to do what needed to be done, saving Dad's life in exchange for giving details about the commanders of the underground operating against the Turks.

Immediately after I met with him, he got on the boat, the same boat in which my love's life had ended and sailed north while I returned home. I am not sure you even felt that I was gone in those hard hours, but it was in that very meeting that dad's life was saved and mine ended.

The next day, the emissary from Damascus arrived. He didn't come to take dad. He came to announce the withdrawal of the order to take him. You all thought it was a miracle from the heavens: "Blessed be the name of the Lord."

Nevertheless, my dear Mother, I knew that it was not God who had saved dad and that it wasn't a miracle that came down from the sky but rather a lowlife traitor who had sold his soul to save his beloved father.

I will never forget the picture in the newspaper with the two bodies dangling from a noose in the main square in Damascus and the cheering crowd around them. The image of those hanged was replaced in my mind with that of Dad. The truth was right there in my face. I have always known – it would be either them or him. I know that there is no forgiveness for what I had done. I shall never forget or accept my actions that will haunt me for the rest of my life.

I wanted to put an end to the anguish, but at the very last minute I came to my senses and chose a different, easy way that might actually be the hard one. In the moment of what would be my greatest crisis, I met people who told me that there was room in the world for forgiveness and for mercy, even for sinners like me. I held onto their words like a lifesaving rope and earned back my life.

I do not know if you will ever show this letter to Dad and I leave that to your discretion, but I do know that when he hears about me, he will cry and tear his shirt in mourning and I pray for him, that his cry would be heard, unlike mine.

I do not have anything left in me to spill my heart out. Please know, Mother, that whatever happens, you, my father, brother, and sister are dear to me and I will love you all until the end of my days.

With much love,
Dudi

***

The letter tore Hannah's soul. She pondered on her son's choice and tormented herself thinking what she would have done in his stead.

Long days she woke up and went to the dairy as if forced, unwillingly and without purpose. One son converted to Christianity, the other immersed in his teachings in Jerusalem, her daughter devoted her days to sewing clothes, and her husband, who was never interested in dairy, did not feel her distress. The economic situation in the country did not agree with her. People were struggling to fulfil their basic needs, and the demand for "Hannah Cheeses" was waning.

One not so bright day, not many months after the British occupied the land, Ali appeared in the barn and informed her that he had come to say goodbye. He told her that the village leaders had reached an agreement with the English and French authorities that they would evacuate the village and re-establish it on the Damascus plain. Ali had become like a son to her. She pressed him to her chest and gathered the rest of the pain and sorrow she had left in her to part with him lovingly.

Within a few days the mud village dwellers packed up their meager belongings on camels and mules, released the water buffalo from the pens, abandoned the village and migrated to the plains of Damascus. The winter rains destroyed most of the huts, and the grim winter that followed flattened the mud village completely. Cyperus, bulrush, and the common reed took over the lands, and the only remnant of the mud village was the mud itself.

Not only did Hannah lose Ali, but also the buffalo milk that gave her products the aroma and flavor that made them famous.

One rather bright day, she called Esther to come to the dairy.

"I decided to close the dairy and remove the barn," she told her.

Esther hugged her mother. She loved her endlessly, but never related to milk and cheese making.

"Are you sure?" she asked, worried more about her mother rather than the dairy business.

"Yes," her mother replied. "The thought crossed my mind many days ago, after Dudi left us, and yet I continued to work in hopes he would come back and help me as always. Nevertheless, he didn't, and now Ali has gone too, and I have no one left to work with..."

Esther collected her mother into her arms. "I'm sorry I didn't help you enough," she cried.

"You shouldn't have helped me," Hannah replied. "I always believed that my children should do what interests them and follow their hearts."

"Yes, I know," Esther replied, reinforcing her hug.

"But I do have one request," Hannah said. "Do you see the six milk jugs in the corner? I ask you to look after them for me. Ali brought them to me from Damascus, and I believe they will come in handy."

"I promise," Esther replied.

***

After seven tumultuous days at sea, Dudi arrived at the port of Southampton in the south of England, where he boarded a train for another four-hour journey to London. He turned to the information post at the train station.

"Waiting for you over there." The information teller pointed to a man standing in the corner in gray clothes and a vicar's white collar. The two marched toward each other.

"David," Dudi reached out his hand.

"Bob," the man replied, shaking his outstretched hand. "Have you ever been to London before?"

"No," David replied, refraining from telling his host that he had never visited London or anywhere else in the world.

"To the theological center," Bob instructed the driver of the carriage after the two boarded.

On their short journey, while the driver maneuvered among the many carriages that filled the streets and cursed the few cars that began to appear on the streets of London, Bob took on the role of the tour guide and explained to the astonished David about the wonderful sights they were passing on their way.

"The Theological Center," or in its full name, "The Theological Center of the Anglican Church," written in prominent letters across the facade of the building, was housed in a mansion built of pink stone. Above the arched entrance swung a large copper cross that blended with the simplicity of the building.

David grabbed his bag and went with Bob into the main hall of the building. The first thing that impressed him was the considerable number of people who huddled in the lobby wearing priests' clothes. In the center of the lobby stood a counter and, on the chair, next to it sat a smiling nun in a starched white dress and a matching habit.

"I brought you a guest," Bob told her.

After David introduced himself to the nun, Bob shook his hand and told him, "My work here is done. Best of luck to you."

Shortly after that, a young priest appeared in the foyer and with a smile, invited David to accompany him. He led him to a side hall.

On one side of the hall David saw classrooms, and on the other side guest rooms. The attendant went with him into an office where a small man was sitting behind a large table. The man stood up to greet him with a kind face and a warm smile.

"Welcome to the theological center," he said and poured him a cup of tea from a white pot resting on the table. "This is place is open to all who want to listen, learn, and understand Christianity without any strings attached. Studies here are open and flexible, and everyone can choose the topics of the lectures and their schedule. Lessons are conducted in classrooms, and when necessary, in the main hall. Each course lasts about a week and ends at the church located here on the premises, as you will learn. "I know you have come from far away, and as part of our hospitality policy, I would like to offer you room and board that include our dining room, which serves food that is said to be not too bad at all."

The host led David to one of the rooms near the office and unlocked the door for him with a large key. The room was simple, but David immediately noticed that it included everything a tired student would need: a wide bed, clean sheets, towels, and toiletries. The restrooms were outside the room, but when he went to take a shower, he noted their cleanliness and the unlimited hot water supply, not exactly the conditions he was used to in the village.

After the shower he went to bed and fell asleep for twelve consecutive hours.

When he woke up, he noticed a copy of *The New Testament* on his bedside table, but what was important to him at that moment was the white pants and the white shirt that were waiting for him in the closet.

"I need to know what one does about dirty laundry here," he said to himself.

He hurried to the dining room, where he made himself a cup of tea and ate a sandwich with cheese and meat. Then he walked to the main hall. The topic of the lecture was: "The Anglican Church as Part of the Christian Faith." The lecturer was a respectable bishop in colorful clothes, who explained about the attributes of the Anglican Church.

David found that under the heading "Christian religion," there are dozens of streams, namely Catholic Protestant and the Anglican churches.

"The Anglican Church is a fairly young church," the bishop said. "It was founded in the sixth century, but it was not until the sixteenth century that it cut itself off from the Church in Rome and its subordination to the pope. One of the reasons for the separation was the approach toward the institution of marriage. While the strict rules of the catholic church prohibited priests from getting married, the Anglican church did not." The bishop looked up at the two women in the audience.

After the lecture, David looked at the list of lectures and to his amazement found a variety of talks related to Judaism and the Land of Israel. Among other things, he signed up to attend courses on the New and Old Testaments, a course on Jesus and the Jews, the Jewish heritage as part of the tenets of the Christian faith, and holy places in the Land of Israel. The course which caused him the greatest astonishment was entitled: "Introduction to the Hebrew Language."

In the first opportunity he had, he made his way to the Hebrew class. To his surprise, the classroom was packed. In his opening remarks, the lecturer said that knowledge of Latin and Hebrew is necessary for any good Christian who wishes to climb the ranks of Christian holiness.

At the end of seven days of lectures, reflections, and conversations with other participants, David saw on the bulletin board an ad regarding a conversion ceremony on the upcoming Sunday open to all who would be interested.

**

The church was full of worshipers. A vicar standing at the entrance invited prospective converts to sit in the front row. Only nine people sat in that row and David was one of them.

After the choir sang hymns and praised Christ, the bishop took to the stage and blessed the nine people so eager to join the Christian faith. One by one the new Christians approached the stage, each receiving a personal blessing from the bishop. A trainee standing by his side held a large silver font adorned with precious stones containing holy water. The bishop dipped his fingers in the water and splashed on the foreheads of the Christians-to-be.

David stepped off the stage without much excitement yet at peace with his decision and his newly-found path.

After everyone had dispersed, one of the priests approached and invited him to the bishop's office. The bishop sat in the office smiling warmly without the purple robe he wore during the ceremony, his head exposed and revealing baldness.

"How are you?" he asked David.

David, puzzled by the very meeting with the Honorable Bishop, replied, "I feel great and thrilled by the experience."

"And what are your plans?" the bishop asked.

"Honestly, I haven't thought about it yet."

"I have a proposal for you." He surprised him. "I would like to suggest you attend seminary."

David was astonished and replied, "I've been a Christian for barely two hours, and you are already suggesting I study for the clergy?"

The bishop responded calmly, "We choose our priests according to their quality and skills."

"What do you know about me?" David inquired.

"Enough to repeat my suggestion. You come from a different culture, and the Anglican Church believes that mixing cultures enriches and deepens faith. Besides, we do not have people in the church who are proficient in the Hebrew language like you. And we have no doubt that you can contribute a lot to the church as a vicar. Take your time, think it over, and let me know in the morning." The bishop rose and shook his hand with encouragement and a sense of partnership.

The next morning, after prayers, David returned to the bishop's office.

The bishop recognized the spark of acceptance in his eyes and said to him with a piercing gaze, "I am glad you have accepted the offer. We would be honored and privileged to have you join priesthood ranks. What we have left to decide is in which path. Every year thirty students are admitted to our seminary. We have two paths, that of community which emphasizes the connection between faith and the individual, and the theological route that is more academic."

David did not need much thought. "I've always been interested in the human connection," he said. "And I have no doubt that the community path suits me better."

"I think you have made a worthy choice," the bishop said contentedly. "I'll take care of everything. Godspeed."

***

The thirty students who began their studies at the Clerical School were a diverse and multinational group. David shared his now upgraded room with a student from the Philippines.

In the first year, all students studied the same classes. They learned about Christianity and its origins, its development, and goals, as well as the independent path of the Anglican Church. In the second year they split up. Twelve students went on the theological route while the rest down the community path.

"A vicar accompanies the believer throughout their entire life," the bishop who was the director of the seminary, said in his introduction. "From one's birth to their funeral prayer, though it may not necessarily be the same priest..." He seasoned his words with a dash of humor.

David was not the institution type, so initially, he was quite apprehensive about studying at the seminary. Curiosity, creativity, independent thinking suited him better. During his school years in the village of Yesodot, he experienced rigor and rigidity. His teacher's word was sacred, and every original thought was suppressed at its inception.

Smiling, David recalled how in one of the classes in the village, the students were asked to show some creativity and draw the rainbow that Noah must have seen when he came out of the ark. The work by Nurit, the obedient and industrious teacher's pet, was pinned up onto the board.

David looked at the colorful painting and said to the teacher, "If this is what the rainbow looked like, why is the color blue not mentioned in the Bible?"

The teacher did not see fit to address the question of the curious student and went on to describe the wonders of the almighty.

Seminary was different. Lessons were based on dialogue, freedom of thought, and respect for the opinion of others. In a course discussing the relationship between Christianity and Judaism, for example, a variety of opinions and thoughts were presented to the students, and lecturers from all walks of life, including the Chief Rabbi of London, presented their positions and beliefs.

At the end of the school day, David would exchange impressions of the day's experiences with Foyo, his roommate from the Philippines. When they left one of the first lessons in the course on Judeo-Christian relations, Foyo turned to him mortified, saying," I must confess. At first, I was a little apprehensive about living with you, because in the Philippines we were taught that the Jews crucified Jesus..."

Sundays were for study and reflection. The students, divided into small teams, moved between the various churches around London and integrated themselves with congregations attending the various masses. During these visits David would study the believers and followed their responses to sermons and prayers. From his observation, he learned of the extent to which the vicar influenced his congregation. He noticed that a cheerful priest who speaks from the heart can shape the congregation and make them follow suit. People of such a community will smile, hum with joy, and return home happy and with strong faith.

Mondays were David's favorite. Free from school and various chores he used to wear his regular clothes, topped with a warm coat according to the season, and set out to roam the streets of London. His favorite places were the green parks and the bustling markets. He found in the parks neither reeds nor Cyperus nor bulrush, however, he did find bright green grass and plenty of water that evoked past memories.

David loved people and he would meet many in the markets. He strolled among them, lingered by the stalls, and listened to their language spoken in local dialect. At the Meisels' house in Yesodot they knew English. It was the legacy of his great-grandmother, who came to Safed from London years ago. Knowing the language was preserving the family heritage, and his mother made sure that all her children learned English. What they did not have time to learn from her, they learned with the help of a private tutor who came to their house twice a week. The English in the market sounded different to that he spoke at home and in the seminary, and he, curious as he was, was happy to enrich his knowledge of its nuances.

The years went by quickly. Beyond theory, seminary students also dabbled in practice, and received guidance as for all expected and unexpected things a vicar may be exposed to during his tenure. A significant chapter was dedicated to the matter of confession.

"This is a whole doctrine," the priest who specialized in confessions said. "And the theory of confession requires many hours of study. Here you will hear lectures from expert speakers on psychology and matters of the soul..."

The curriculum also included courses in social work and basic economics to prepare the trainees for their tenure as leaders and teachers in the community. At the end of his studies, David felt that he was mature and ready for the task he undertook.

***

Thirty vicars in training sat on two long benches in front of the church, excited to finally be ordained. The hall was full of family members, seminary teaching staff, and the trainees. The ceremony was presided over by the director of the Theological Seminary, and the guest of honor was the Bishop of London.

One by one, the graduates were called to the stage, there stood the bishop and in front of him a font of holy water brought from the place of Christ's baptism. The director of the seminary called the names of the graduates. They would approach the bishop, who dipped his hand in the font and marked the sign of the cross on each of their foreheads. After that, they would each approach the director of the seminary who placed the clerical collar. At the end of the ceremony the bishop greeted the new vicars, who had just joined the ranks of the church.

CHAPTER 5 – BLACK EAGLE

"Where is Timbuktu? What is the highest place in the world? What bird spends most of its time flying?" These were some of the ninety questions the trivia host held in his hand. He kept the hundredth question in a sealed envelope in his back pocket.

"Never let a contestant win the first prize of one-thousand pounds," was the production's instruction after the presenter was once caught plotting with one of the contestants to share the winnings.

Just as the gameshow host did not know the answer to the question 'where is Timbuktu?' David did not know the answer to where Black Eagle was, though he was just about to find out. The question came up at the end of a very exciting day.

The eighteen graduates of the community program of the Theology Seminary for Christian Studies stood thrilled before the dean's office, where he was hosting the bishop who came especially for the graduation ceremony. Chambers were ready to notify the young priests where in England they would be posted.

Excited and nervous, David entered the chamber, shook hands with the dean and the bishop, and heard the bishop inform him in his authoritative voice, "David Meisels, after in-depth discussions we have decided to send you to serve as vicar at the Black Eagle Church. May God be with you."

Neither the bishop nor the dean knew where called "Black Eagle" was, but David saw it as a secondary matter. The sense of mission filled him and he expected to arrive quickly at the church he was entrusted with.

After parting with his classmates, he turned to Lilly, the institute's eternal secretary. Her glasses were slung over the tip of her nose, and in her hand, she held a large white envelope bearing his name.

"I see that you have been appointed vicar of Black Eagle. Such an honor. According to my notes, the previous vicar was abruptly transferred to somewhere in north of England. The reasons were omitted though. He was instructed to leave the keys in the flowerpot near the entrance."

"I'm sure I'll be fine," David replied firmly. "But where's Black Eagle?"

Lilly was mortified. They unfolded the map of England and searched, but the name "Black Eagle" did not appear on the map. Lilly scattered the papers and rummaged through, finally letting out a sigh of relief. "I see the place is somehow connected to New Castle..."

With the confidence of a twenty-five-year-old, David informed her, "I will find the place."

He shook her hand, grabbed the envelope and his backpack that contained his few belongings, and boarded a carriage to London Central Station. At the station, he was informed that the soonest train to New Castle would depart today, Wednesday, at noon. To his question, the man at the window responded that the trip would last about eight hours.

David arrived in New Castle that night. The station was empty. He spent the night on one of the benches in the station hall, and the next morning rushed to one of the counters and asked for a ticket to Black Eagle.

The teller stared at him in surprise as if he had ordered a ticket to the moon, however, luckily for David, after a lengthy inspection, informed him that he had found the place. But, he added, the train stops there only twice a week, and the next trip was not until Saturday afternoon.

Disappointed yet happy, David spent his days at the train station until Saturday morning, when he boarded the train, which would stop at Black Eagle on its way to Glasgow.

The wobbly train ride lasted about six hours. When the announcer called out the name of the impending stop, David went into the bathroom, put on a starched white shirt he had taken out of his backpack, fastened the clerical collar, and waited for the glorious arrival at Black Eagle.

"Next stop: 'Black Eagle!'" He heard the announcement.

The train creaked, and David jumped off the step even before the train made it to a full stop, for fear of missing the station. He was the only one to get off the train. After the train set off on its way, the young priest found himself in a clover field bisected by a railroad. A faded sign, slumped on its side, read the letters B... K ..GLE. There was nothing but the sign.

The surrounding fields were covered in black dust. In the distance, black hills could be seen and apart from them, nothing. Yet nothing could hinder his happiness, not even the fact that he did not know where to go, and where Black Eagle was.

In the distance, in the direction of the black hills, a cart drawn by an old, tired horse appeared. The elongated-faced driver who looked somewhat like his tired horse approached him with his wagon.

"Sir, where is Black Eagle?" David asked.

The driver turned his face toward David and did not look surprised at the sight of the priest landing on him from heaven. He pointed his thumb in the opposite direction and hurried his horse on their way.

True to the detailed instructions he had received, David walked the path between the fields, toward the black hills. After about an hour of walking he finally reached his destination – the village of Black Eagle.

The village was actually two short rows of small, faded houses with red, tiled roofs. In front of each house was a small garden, all boasting carnations and rose bushes. Seeing that this is a happy community, David rejoiced inside. He noticed that behind each house was a black mound. After the mass I will find out the meaning of these heaps, he noted to himself.

The church could not be missed. Its stone structure was large and impressive, making the houses next to it look remarkably small. The church building was also faded, but the large cross in front of it was bright white. Indeed, great are the deeds of the Lord, David smiled with delight. Adjacent to the church was a small house. Nervous and with his stomach convulsing, David approached the large clay container at the entrance to the house. The key was right where he expected it to be.

The two-room house was lightly furnished. It was clear that its last occupant was a remorseful person. The large wooden cross hanging on one of the walls was the only decoration in the house. The main item in the room was a wooden table and on it, a blue ceramic bowl with a large black key with three serrated teeth in its center. A wooden bed stood to the side of the room with a mattress stuffed with seaweed, covered with a light sheet and a rolled-up blanket made of fleece. In the center of the room stood a charcoal-filled heater. Apparently, the previous tenant had no shortage of charcoal and David was thankful for his good fortune.

In the corner of the room, he discovered a cooking area, a cracked sink, a kettle, and a cooking pot on a charcoal stove. Above the pot hung a set of cutleries, the kind one would find in a flea market. He also found jars filled with coffee powder, brown sugar, and dried white leaf savory. By the bed was an entrance to a narrow stall served as a toilet and bathroom.

David took off his priest's outfit to hang on a broken wooden hanger by the narrow bathroom. He went into the shower, the icy water reminded him to turn on the heater placed on the charcoal stove. To his delight, after the shower he found a box of canned beans and musty lentils in the pantry. He took some dry stalks of the white savory and soaked them in a cup of boiling water. The hot tea, the hunger that was since nourished and the heat that spread throughout the room made his heart cheer.

He went to bed and immediately sank into a deep sleep, not before thanking the Lord for all his ways and the momentous day ahead.

***

David drew back the curtain. The tall wall of the church could be seen in the darkness, blocking any other view out of the window. It was foggy outside. He took the round watch out of the pocket of his trousers and realized that he had three hours left before mass.

The thought of mass sparked his excitement and enthusiasm.

He pulled out folded sheets of paper from his bag and began to read out loud,. "My fellow congregants! I, Vicar David Meisels, was sent here by the church on God's mission, to be your faithful, humble servant, through joy and in sorrow..."

David knew the text by heart. He had written and deleted his sermon back and forth dozens of times.

He made notes to himself where to raise and when to lower his voice, when he should look up to the sky, and when to direct his gaze at the devout believers. Hours were spent practicing at the theological institute as part of the mandatory course on rhetoric, and now was the time to put what he learned to use. No more group training among friends, no more tutorials and examinations by instructors, but standing independently in front of an enthusiastic crowd of believers, who would come to hear the new vicar's sermon.

Time went by slowly. David sipped another cup of tea; put on the white shirt that he had brushed thoroughly after the walk across the clover field. He combed his hair in front of the large mirror hanging in the bathroom, proudly placed the clerical collar around his neck, put on the priest's robe, and took the black key on his way to church, not before taking one more pleased look in the mirror.

The fog faded a little, but visibility was still limited, and one could barely see the nearby village houses. With five determined steps David reached the heavy wooden door of the church, stuck the notched key in the door lock, turned it three times, and opened it lowly with a jarring, rusty creak.

The inside of the house of God was shrouded in ancient gloom and the smell of mold. In front of the entrance stood a low stage with an altar. Behind it, on the tall wall hung the tormented figure of Messiah nailed to a cross. The priest's pulpit stood by the alter where he would deliver his sermon.

From the entrance to the altar stood two rows of rigid wooden benches, covered in dust that not even the shadowy gloom could obscure. At five to eight, an hour before mass, David went down to the front door and opened it wide. An open door gives believers a sense of home, he told himself.

At exactly eight o'clock he pulled a rope that dangled down at the end of the stage, and the ringing of the bells filled the church, spreading throughout the village. A cool breeze swirled through the open door. David loved the sound of the bells, which was gentle to his ears but dominant enough to wake up the last of the villagers. While the bells rang, he lit the thurible, and the burning incense slightly dissolved the moldy scent. He had less than an hour left for the big event.

David went to the stand and out of pure urge, took the white pages out of his pocket and began to read out loud, "My fellow congregants..." But then immediately folded the papers and stuffed them back into his pocket.

Not only did he know his entire speech by heart, but he also remembered his informed decision not to deliver a sermon from paper.

At nine o'clock he stared at the front door and loosened his arms, preparing for a hug he would send in the air to the stream of believers on their way in.

No one came.

***

The bright eyes of nine o'clock seemed filled with disappointment at twelve. Perhaps members of the parish are not aware that the church has reopened, he thought. Next Sunday's mass will be filled, he reassured himself. After three frustrating hours of standing behind the podium, he walked off with aching muscles, shut the heavy door, turned the key three times to lock it, and turned to the only road in the village to demonstrate his presence.

True to the belief he had cultivated throughout his years of seminary, David had decided that he would be a new brand of vicar. None of those sermons copied from the textbook, no more monotonous reading, not a condescending vicar but rather a vicar that creates a sense of trust and closeness with his parish, heart-to-heart, eye-to-eye.

The street was empty and at the end very end of it was a different-looking one-story building. David approached it and saw that weeds were growing all over. Signs were affixed to both doors of the building. One: "Post office – open every day between twelve and one o'clock (except Sundays)," and the other: "Grocery store and spare parts – open (except Sundays) between ten and two o'clock." On the third door frame hung a stuffed deer head with long curved horns, sipping a beer from a can.

Disappointed and hungry, David turned on his heel back to church.

Suddenly, the door with the stuffed deer opened and a huge, red-headed man with red cheeks and green shorts dangling from his massive belly, revealing two white legs appeared.

The man looked at the vicar in shock and asked, "What are you doing here, Father? Can I help with anything?"

"Yes," David replied. "I'm the new vicar and I came to meet people and also buy something to eat."

The giant man looked at him amused and said, "People are in their homes. This is their chance to rest from working in the mines. But come at night." He winked at him. "Our pub is quite jolly."

David was uncomfortable by the offer. "I shall not come to the pub, but you are welcome to visit the church on Sunday."

"Why would I go there?" The giant laughed. "But wait a minute..." He entered the pub and returned a moment later with an old rolled-up newspaper containing half a loaf of bread and a slice of cheese. "So that you have something to eat until tomorrow." He generously sent him on his way.

That's a good start, David noted. He has a deep baritone voice, suitable for singing Psalm hymn twenty-nine.

David spent the rest of his day organizing and cleaning his new home. He arranged the holy books and placed the Old Testament next to the bowl on the table.

The next day he returned to church. The air inside was clearer, but the dust seemed heavier. In the center of the church, he saw the confessional. The booth was divided into two, separate exits for each section to prevent the confessor and the priest from meeting face-to-face. David entered the booth. On the vicar's chair, he found a bucket with a rag inside it, and a mop next to it. The confessional was parted by a wooden wall with a perforated lattice in the center, and a high wooden chair in each.

David recalled the confession workshop. The student learned that the confessional must be spartan and give a sense of loneliness and sadness. It must also be dim and detached from external noises and give the confessor a sense of sanctity. The confessor must be attentive and focused, and not be distracted by material matters.

David took out the bucket and the mop and began to clean and polish both parts of the confessional. Once he had finished, he said to himself, "Now the confessional is up to par and ready to fulfil its purpose."

He devoted the rest of the week to cleaning the church. With his bare hands, he polished the floors, washed and dried the benches, and paid special attention to the altar and the pulpit.

On Sunday at eight o'clock in the morning the bells rang, and the incense rustled. The church door was wide open. The fog outside had mostly dissipated, and light clouds dotted the sky. A day that is all good, David thought. He decided to get off of the stage and wait at the broad entrance.

At about nine o'clock in the morning a woman appeared at the door. She wore a loose floral dress and a wide-brimmed black hat, adorned with a gray ribbon on the front.

David invited her with great excitement to the first row and stood behind the podium.

After some hesitation, he began, "My fellow believer…"

For about forty minutes he delivered his dream sermon, alternating enthusiastic gazes between the person on the bench and his God in heaven. He finished the sermon with the words, "May God be with you."

The lady stood up, took off her hat, bowed her head and received the communion wafer from his hands. After she finished chewing the holy biscuit, she turned to the priest, "I need to make a confession!"

David welcomed his good fortune: here he is about to conduct the first confession of his life! He accompanied the lady to the confessional and sat down in his narrow, high chair.

The confessor sat in the same chair on the other side of the partitioned booth, all in accordance with the rules.

"What is your name, my child?" David asked the confessor, who was twice his age.

"My name is Joyce," she replied.

"The merciful and forgiving God is waiting for you, Joyce, and invites you to tell him all that is on your heart."

"I cheated on my husband," she told him in a low, tormented voice.

David was astonished. During their Confession Theory course, students were told that twenty-three percent of the confessions were about personal issues, but what amazed him was the bluntness and directness with which things were said.

"I hear and understand that you are sorry for what you have done, and I am sure that the merciful God will forgive you and bless you and your husband with a good life," he delivered a message of forgiveness and love.

She stood up on her feet and before leaving the confessional she said, "I would like to book a confession for next Monday as well."

"Why on Monday?"

"Because every Sunday my husband goes to the pub to get drunk, and I sneak out the house to meet John in an abandoned warehouse near the mine."

He did not learn about such a situation in his course. "I beg your pardon?" He was astounded. "Do you expect me to give you the okay for an intended sin?"

"If you knew Willie, my husband, you wouldn't be surprised," she declared and left the confessional.

***

At ten o'clock Monday morning, David arrived at the empty grocery store. Few food products were scattered on the shelves as well as some snacks inside sacks placed on the floor. Behind the counter stood a smiling young woman who was happy to greet the first customer of the day.

"How can I help you, Father?" she asked.

"I'm the new vicar here and I came to buy various food products."

"You see we don't have much of a selection but if you are missing something I'd be happy to make an order from New Castle especially for you."

"Thank you kindly," he said. "But before that, please tell me something… why do I not see people on the street?"

The young woman laughed with a mouth full of teeth and said, "If you want to meet people, go to the mine. They work there day in, day out."

After filling his shopping cart with basic products, David saw a bar of chocolate on the counter. "I'd like that as well," he told the saleslady and she looked at him suspiciously. "Is there a problem?" he asked.

"No..." she replied reluctantly. "The other priest also bought the first packet—"

"So why the hesitation?"

"Two years ago, my husband brought two packets of chocolate from New Castle. The first was bought by the priest who was here before you, but when my husband found out what he did with the chocolate, he refused to sell him the second packet, nor did he agree to sell him sweets that children like."

"And what happened in the end?"

"I don't know if it was the end or the beginning, but a year ago my husband died of pneumonia he caught down in the mine, and the vicar refused to hold a funeral service for him in church."

David was appalled and his tongue cleaved to the roof of his mouth.

"I'm sorry to have embarrassed you," said the women. "You can, of course, take the bar of chocolate, but know that it has expired, and slander is very dominant on that street."

David paid the bill and before leaving the store he turned to the young woman. "I have two questions. The first, what happened to the priest? And the second, what is Joyce's address?"

"About six months ago, one of the mothers filed a complaint with the bishop, and one day we found out that both the church and the vicarage were locked. They said they moved him far away, but no one wanted to tell us where to. We have only one Joyce in the village, and she lives three houses away, on the left side of the street. You'll recognize it by the hyacinth blooming in front of the house. You seem like a nice young vicar to me, and I'm sure you'll remember what I told you earlier."

David skipped over the hyacinth house and continued directly to the church, where he sat on the priest's chair near the altar. Sweat covered the back of his neck. A beginner's mistake, he thought. Bought the second packet of chocolate and asked for Joyce's address...

He considered what the head of the institute said in his concluding speech: "Studies are important, experience even more, but the most essential thing is common sense."

He took the chocolate out of his robe, placed it on the altar, hoping that would not constitute blasphemy, and began to contemplate with his common sense.

***

Six in the morning is an unpleasant hour in Black Eagle. The mist refuses to end the night shift and gloom and darkness prevails. Next to one of the black heaps, not far from the church, a lantern flickered, slightly illuminating a small pavilion where an older man was sitting and trying to warm up his hands with a cup of boiling hot tea. Two men with their calloused hands and black furrows in their fingers were waiting for him curled up in heavy coats. He got up, made them sign a form of some sort, gave each of them a pickaxe and shovel and told them to wait by the elevator nearby. David approached him, shivering from the debilitating cold.

"How can I help you?"

"I'm looking for a job in the mine."

"Do you have experience working in a mine?" He looked skeptically at David's white hands.

"No."

"No problem," the man relented. "We don't need experience. Do what the other two are doing. Just know that the shift is until six in the evening. Wages are twenty pence a strip."

"That would do for me," David replied without knowing what that meant. He signed a form, received a pickaxe and shovel as well as a used orange miner suit and helmet.

"Over there." The man directed with his chin.

The new laborer joined the two waiting, and together the three descended in an elevator to the depths of the mine.

When the elevator stopped, they boarded a conveyor that led them to shaft number one. A tunnel ran through the depths of the mine, with a narrow track in the center and on it, a conveyor. On both sides of the tracks were niches shaped in the rock, and next to each – an empty container.

The two workers stood, each in front of a different niche, and began chiseling. After accumulating a sufficient amount of coal, they would pick it up and pour it into the container.

David stood in front of a vacant niche between the other two and began to chisel. The tunnel was dark. A row of lanterns illuminated it faintly, and a separate lantern hung over each niche. An air duct designed to dilute the compressed air in the tunnel descended from the ceiling. The cold was unbearable. David wondered when his body would turn into a block of ice.

The quarrying in the rock seemed to him like an easy job, but after a few minutes his hands became stiff and heavy. The rock turned out to be quite stubborn. The hacking did not seem to bother it very much. Pains plagued his body from his legs up to his back.

"At least I'm not as cold as I was," he mumbled to himself.

The noise of the pickaxes broke the silence. None of his co-workers said anything. Their sealed faces were turned to a black wall of coal. They deftly tapped the rock, occasionally stopping to scoop the coal up into their containers.

David's container remained almost empty. When he hit the wall in a rage and tried to extract coal from the rock, he discovered that the stone tendon was cut along its entire length, which had hindered quarrying. I should ask for a different niche, he told himself.

At noon he put down his pickaxe and sat with his co-workers on a nearby wooden beam. A rumbling sound came from a distance. A small tram passed over the tracks containing wooden bowls. Each of the three took a bowl. In his bowl David found lukewarm porridge, dull in color and in flavor. Unfortunately, he did not notice that his colleagues also took a spoon, so he had to eat directly from the bowl.

True to the goal he set for himself, David turned to the two next to him. "Can I ask you something?"

Their angry glares answered his question. You can't ask anything. It's not personal, he thought, neither of them exchanged a single word the entire day. The thirty-minute break had ended, and they each returned to hacking and David to his aching.

At exactly six o'clock a freight car approached. An unknown figure sat on it. What set him apart was the layer of coal that covered his body. Using a hand crane, the coal man lifted the container next to one of the workers and poured its contents into the large container on the tram. He marked the height of the coal with white chalk and wrote in a small notebook he held in his hand. "One pound twenty pence."

The second miner was more efficient. "One pound forty," he informed him, writing in his notebook.

When he got to David, he raised his head for the first time and said, "Twenty pence."

The coal man bowed his head and propelled the tram on its way, while David took the elevator to the entrance of the mine. He returned the pickaxe and shovel to a nearby tool shed, left the overalls on his body, and announced, "I'll be coming back tomorrow."

He managed to open the door of the house and take off his mud-covered shoes, but no more than that. He fell onto the bed in his dirty clothes, and only toward six in the morning did he wake up and shower. He ate a thin slice of toast, sipped a cup of tea, and rushed to the mine.

This time they gave him a different niche, left of his colleague from yesterday. His pain intensified, but the hope in his heart gave him the encouragement he needed. Today I will earn eighty pence, he told himself.

At twelve o'clock in the afternoon the porridge wagon arrived. Experience had taught David to take the wooden spoon as well.

"My name is Willie, and I know who you are."

David was sure the mine was going to swallow him. The man can speak... he stared at him.

"What brings you to the mine?" Willie asked.

"I came to learn about the livelihoods of my parish and bring them closer to God."

"What God are you talking about? Here, fifty feet below the ground, there is no God, and I'm sure he's not up there either."

"God is everywhere. I would be happy to introduce him to you."

"There is no God," Willie insisted. "If there was a God, he would not have sent me to a mine at the age of twelve and my father at the age of ten. You know, my grandfather, whom I never knew was sent to work here at the age of eight."

Silence returned to the tunnel. David felt something hard in his pocket and took out the packet of chocolate. The other two looked stunned.

"What is that? Chocolate?" Willie asked.

"Yes, it's chocolate," David replied.

He divided the packet into three and gave each one his share. Willie held the chocolate with excitement, breaking a piece from the edge and putting it in his mouth. His eyes closed and his mouth tightened, savoring the moment.

"The last time I tasted this chocolate was when I married Joyce, thirty years ago."

David wondered if he did, in fact, notice a tear in one eye.

Willie put the remaining piece in his mouth and whispered, "Maybe there is a God after all..."

At six o'clock David ascended to earth. He returned the tools and the orange overalls. He announced that he would not be returning to work, and asked to divide his wages, which had already amounted to one pound, between his shift mates. At home, tired as he was the day before yet still on his feet, he washed his body, put on his night clothes and before sinking into deep sleep, contemplated the ways of the Lord.

***

The days went by. David recalled the proverb: "There is one thing that cannot be stopped in life, and that is time."

Sunday had arrived.

At eight o'clock the bells rang, the scent of incense prevailed over the smell of coal, and the front door was open. A few minutes before nine o'clock three people entered the church: a woman dressed in her Sunday Best and a gracious hat on her head, and with her, Joyce holding Willie's arm.

"My fellow worshippers..." David began and immediately abandoned the wording he had prepared and trailed off about giving and friendship, about love and hope. He spoke quietly and humbly. He even gave up his timed gaze to the heavens and to the figure of Jesus behind him.

At the end of his sermon, he invited the small congregation to taste the sacramental bread. Joyce was last.

After receiving the round wafer, she raised her head and whispered softly to the vicar, "I'd like to cancel tomorrow's confession."

In one of the next Sundays the church was half full. At the end of the ceremony, one member of the parish approached David.

"I'm the manager down at the mine. I came to thank you for the new spirit you have brought into the mine and for the increase in productivity. Can I do anything for you?"

David did not hesitate and whispered something in the mine manager's ear, who smiled at him with understanding.

A week later, the train stopped at Black Eagle station and large crates were loaded on to two horse-drawn carriages. The following Sunday, church attendees were surprised to see that the hard church bleachers, were replaced by new pews more agreeable to their bottoms. The old benches were handed over to the village carpenter who took them apart and at the request of the vicar, given away to members of the community free of charge.

The number of churchgoers multiplied. The positive gale that blew from the church gave villagers optimism and hope. The post office increased its hours to two a day, an attempt to cope with the load of letters sent to the parish, with the question: "What is happening over there?"

The jolly young woman who ran the grocery shop also increased her business and was now debating whether to keep the shop open on Sundays as well.

The pub was bustling with new life, and the man with the baritone voice happily welcomed the women who came to share a Guinness with the men.

Another Sunday came, and the church was full! Before the sermon started, a respectable man approached David and said, "I was sent to convey a message to the workers, and I want you to be the first to know about it. Management has decided on its own initiative to raise the wages of the workers in the mine by another twenty pence per strip."

That morning David opened the sermon with the words, "Dear members of our community, Hallelujah!!! The prophet Habakkuk said, 'Wait for it; it will surely come.'"

Yet another fully packed Sunday arrived, and everyone was wearing white shirts that had recently been purchased at the grocery shop, which had also opened a clothing department. David started with a sermon, original and appropriate to circumstances, as always.

Out of the corner of his eye he saw two men at the end of the hall, near the entrance. One wore a pristine priest's outfit while the other, vibrant bishop's clothing with a matching headdress. Since he did not want to stop the ceremony, he decided he would approach the guests at the end.

When he had finished his sermon, David moved the pulpit revealing the new church choir in a grand world premiere. The choir consisted of four women and four men all dressed in white shirts, and dark skirts on the women and dark pants on the men.

Out of the choir stepped out a tall man, and in a spectacular baritone voice, which would usually be echoed between the walls of his pub, began to sing, "Out of the depths I cry to you, O Lord"

The rest of the choir stepped forward and sang hymn Psalm 130.

"Let your ears be attentive to my cry for mercy"

It was an incredible sight. The entire congregation stood up with tears in their eyes and sang words begging for mercy along with the choir.

"O Lord, hear my voice"

When all the exhilaration had subsided, David rushed to receive his guests, but the two had already disappeared. When he asked the people sitting in the back pews where the distinguished guests had gone, Joyce approached and told him that during the prayer they started crying. Probably mortified, they got on a waiting carriage and left in a hurry...

Two weeks later a special courier came to David. At that point, the train would stop at the station six times a week. The envoy invited him to a meeting with the Bishop of New Castle.

The bishop welcomed him warmly, and after exchanging the usual greetings, he lay all his cards on the table.

"We are a big city with a lot of trouble. In recent years we have noticed a disconnect between the church and the parish, which is evident by a steady decline in the number of church visitors and the number of believers seeking confession. We have been following your work in Black Eagle and even the diocese in London have commended you for the deep transformation you've managed to generate in the community's relationship with the church. Our archdeacon has recently passed away, and we think it's time to make a serious change. We consulted with the Archbishop of London, and he has given us his blessing to offer you the position of Archdeacon of St. Michael's Church in New Castle.

"I will be honest with you and add I will ask you not to cling to the word offer. In fact, the decision has already been made and you shall be assuming the position shortly. Please do not see us as too rough on you; I want to tell you that based on your personality and independent thought, you would be at liberty to make your own decisions regarding your relationship with the congregation, while upholding the Christian values of church, naturally."

David spent the next two weeks in prayers and farewell meetings with believers and non-believers in Black Eagle, inviting everyone to pray with him to the same God, only in a different church.

***

"We don't sell Guinness"
"We don't sell Newcastle"
"We won't sell Betty"

David could not decipher the meaning of the signs on the front of the Grainger market. He took his little notebook out of his back pocket and made a note to find out what the signage poets meant.

Located in the old city of Newcastle, the market was crowded with people in the afternoon. The main portion of the market was comprised of fish stalls which dominated the smells and colors of the entire area. Fruit and vegetable stalls were scattered in other areas of the market. While the fishmongers were mostly men, the rest of the sellers were women wearing long farming clothes and bright-colored kerchiefs, offering some of their best produce picked the previous day from fields around the city. Before dawn, they would make their way to the market in a long convoy.

David left the bustling part of the market and turned to it eastern quarter. That district, with its many shops and strange signs, was closed during those hours. He crossed the quaint signpost and in one of the alleys turned to Quayside. The street stretches along the entire north bank of the Tyne River. On the bank of the broad river, he found a stone bench and sat down to rest his tired feet and admire the spectacular view.

Dozens of freight ships sailed on the river before him, many carrying coal mined in the large mines scattered in the area, to the large port in the North Sea, which was an hour's sailing distance from the city. Other ships floated on the water after unloading their cargo, and headed in the opposite direction, for an endless cycle of loading and unloading.

Not far from where he was seated another, smaller port, used mainly by fishermen who would catch their trawl in the North Sea. The port bustled with fishing boats and the fishermen traded with fishmongers along the wharf. The fish that dominated the noisy exchange was the halibut. The large fish were placed in wheelbarrows and from there transported to the fish stalls at Grainger Market.

The fish stalls were quite the attraction at the local market. By the massive halibut piles, which would reach the height of ten feet tall and weighing around six hundred pounds, were heaps of glistening herring, mackerel, salmon, and other sea fish, and next to all these stood countless food stalls selling roasted, fried, baked, pickled, grilled, and live fish – anything the human stomach can contain and everything the nose can smell.

Anyone visiting Grainger Market or the flea market that was a part of it, in search of an old Scottish bagpipe or a bottle made of antique Irish glass, could not help busting their top at the fish market that was known all over the entire kingdom.

The activity in and around the river was dizzying and fascinating, but at one point David decided it was time to return to St. Michael's Cathedral, which overlooked the city on the other bank of the Tyne.

After evening prayers, David took off his priest's outfit and returned to the Old City. It seemed to him that for a moment he was in the wrong place. The area was completely different. The vegetable market was deserted. The farmers were all gone, and the wooden stalls were covered with thick sheets of cloth. The large crowd that had been fondling cauliflower, potatoes, and other fruits and vegetables all day, was nowhere to be seen.

At the end of the market, the city's cleaning teams were gearing up to clean the garbage heaps from the ground. The fish stalls were gone yet a strong smell lingered in the air. David wrote in his notebook that he should find out what the stall owners did with the fish they did not have time to sell during the day.

Darkness covered the city. David turned east, toward the river. The Strange Signs Quarter, as he called the eastern quarter of the market in his notebook, was now a bright, colorful, and bustling area. Many people crowded the streets holding large glasses of beer. Voices and drunken cheers filled the streets. All the places that were shut during the afternoon became well-lit pubs and restaurants buzzing with hungry people. At the entrance of many places stood women who, if their dress and manners were not enough to attest to their occupation, said overt words of temptation to people going by that would remove any doubt.

David was in shock. He had never seen or imagined such images. As he walked through the crowded alleys, he tried to shake off the pestering women and the crowd that threatened to run over him. In a side alley he came across a sign: "**We don't sell Guinness**"

The sign, which had been off since noon, was now twinkling in a dim light. The dusty shutter was gone. David entered a bustling and noisy hall filled with men and women celebrating and rejoicing. It was the first time in his life that he had visited such a place. Amid the loud noise he could not hear the question poking in his head: What would a priest be doing at a brewery?

Slowly, he finally got used to the noise, and to his dismay began to like the sights around him. He could barely find a seat by the long counter. On the wall in front of it stood beer kegs and in front of them an inscription: "**New Castle Beer**" Below the caption appeared a large, rhombus, blue logo. On a wooden rack rested rows of beer glasses designed in a style that David had never seen before. They had a wide rim, a narrow waist, and an extra-wide bottom.

After a while he took to deepen his acquaintance with the place, a short waiter turned to him and asked, "What about you, sir?"

David was mortified. He wondered if the church guidelines forbade him to drink beer. He pondered over the troubling question, and to get rid of the annoying waiter who stared at him with demanding eyes, he let out, "A glass of water."

The waiter glared at him and angrily said, "You'll be asking for a Guinness soon, fucking Irish git." He disappeared in search of agreeable customers.

David thought he did not understand the words. His friends at St. Michael had explained that in and around New Castle there is a large community of Geordies, people who speak Geordie, a local native slang of the English language. This dialect is difficult to understand for any English person by birth, they said, let alone for those for whom English was not their mother tongue. On second thought, he recalled the waiter's look of horror and decided that the problem was probably not in the language, but in the fact that it was not wanted there. He left the pub.

Across the street he noticed another bright spot with a twinkling inscription: "**We don't sell New Castle**" He crossed the street and entered the pub.

"Half a pint on the house," said the bartender, a tall man with a sloping belly, red cheeks, and a prominent Irish accent. He spotted the new customer and placed before David a large glass of Guinness. The glass was different from that in the neighboring pub. It had a narrow rim that widened toward the bottom.

The pub was half empty. David and his pint were the only ones present at the counter. The bartender, somewhat bored and or perhaps just curious, approached him. "Are you new in town?"

"Do you know all of your customers?" David was astonished.

"I know all the Irish in town, they come only to me for their drinks and clearly, you are not Irish."

David saw the bartender's kindness or boredom as an opportunity to ask," What are those strange signs out there about Newcastle and Guinness?"

The bartender laughed and his belly wobbled. "My father and I wanted to open up an Irish pub down at Grainger Market and when the pub across from us heard, they warned us not to sell Newcastle beer. We found it funny but a day before we opened, someone had broken in and trashed the place. That same night, someone burned the other pub. I don't know who destroyed ours or who burned theirs. They don't either. But one thing is for sure, they've learned not to mess with the Irish.

"After both pubs were renovated, they hung a sign saying they don't sell Guinness. It only helped us because all the Irish customers came to us, and they were getting only the Geordies. But we had to maintain our Irish pride, so we put a sign up saying we don't sell Newcastle. Which is not true. Would you like a Newcastle instead of your Guinness?"

David didn't want either, he just wanted a glass of water, however, he was afraid to ask.

"I see," he said. "But why does the other pub have a sign up that says, 'we won't sell Betty?'"

The bartender choked with laughter and replied, "Why are you asking me? Ask them."

David seized the moment when a new guest entered the pub to get away. He left the Guinness and the glass of water he did not receive on the counter, and went out into the street, to the nearby pub, which carried the sign: "**We won't sell Betty**"

Behind the heavy door were walls lined with bright red cloths, a golden ceiling, and dim lighting. On the stained carpet there stood a table. On the armchair behind it sat a blonde woman with blue eyes highlighted by bold eyeliner, and glorious marble breasts exposed for all to see. David noticed a small black spot on one of her blue eyes.

At the end of the foyer, through a door leading to a large hall, David managed to see men and women part naked, kissing, hugging, and celebrating life.

The woman examined the guest. "Him? Her? Couples? A Threesome?" she questioned.

Shamed and shocked, David managed to say, "I just came in to find out why Betty is not being sold..."

"And you are?" she asked.

"I am a priest," the answer escaped his lips.

The hostess burst into rolling laughter that vibrated the marble twins and revealed two gleaming rows of teeth.

"These past few months we have had twenty-three priests, two bishops, one archbishop, one Shakespeare, King George, a horse and four boys who didn't have enough time to prepare their cover story. Don't worry, everyone here stays anonymous."

"But what about Betty?" he asked.

The hostess stopped laughing and said, "I like you, so I'll tell you. I'm Betty, the owner of the place, and of all the women in the pub I'm the only one not for sale, and I want everyone to know that."

David stared at her and felt himself lose his mind and go into complete shock. He was stunned by the erupting femininity standing in front of him, and by his own self. Tamara's death was for him not only the loss of love, but also the loss of excitement and passion. His studies at the seminary and his work as a vicar suited him. The women he met were integrated into the world of repression in which he lived. No more love, thrills, or sex, but rather that of believers in need of help and a connection with God.

Waves of sensuality flowed into his eyes, and to his amazement he felt a tight awakening in his loins. She stood near him with her white face, blue eyes, reddish hair, and soft, sensual lips, yet what fascinated him was the cleavage that revealed her white, peaked, firm breasts that subdued his soul.

Betty saw his look and caught his excitement. From years spent in her line of work, she had met men of all kinds, though in the eyes of the handsome and tall young man she noticed something else: juvenile passion and a message of honesty and benevolence. She grabbed his arm and pulled him into a narrow side room that was adjacent to the reception area, where she held the back of his neck and clung to him with her entire body.

David felt her heavy breasts pressed against his chest, her clenched belly and tongue penetrating his mouth and swirling with his.

He was just about to faint, and before his knees gave in, she pulled her tongue out, detached herself from him, collected her breasts and said, "Go. I will come to visit you."

David left. With his weakened knees and hazy eyes, he navigated his emptied body to the church.

***

David was lying on his bed in his humble room in St. Michael's Church with his head spinning. The church was a massive structure designed to emphasize the greatness of God. The walls of the hall were covered with sketches depicting the life of Jesus, along with remarkable sculptures, and wood carvings. On the other side of the entrance stood the altar that stretched across the entire hall and above it, arches that led the eyes to the painting of Messiah that covered the entire wall. Between the entrance and the altar was a thick rope separating the congregation from areas restricted to clergy only.

David knew the dispute among the sages of the Anglican Church. Some argued that external signs help a person to understand the soul, and some believed that the soul is more important than the symbol. The compromise, David realized, was found in the design of the meager room allotted to his residence on the second floor of the church, which was far from all the splendor radiated by the building.

This room was one out of an entire row of rooms on that floor. The first, more spacious room was for the head of the church. The other eight bedrooms, modest and ascetic, were used by the vicars who served in the church. And at the very end were the two dormitories of the vicars in training.

The trainees were the bread and butter of the churches. They were seminary students, who were required to intern for a year. Students would compete for a slot according to the prestige of the parish and the degree of its benefit for their future. The ten clergymen in training privileged to be stationed at St. Michael's Church had considered themselves lucky, while the church leaders saw them as servants who were at their command day and night.

Among the duties assigned to the trainees was to ensure the regular supply of holy water, which was a much needed and sought-after commodity in the church. The holy water had many degrees of holiness. Some were brought from springs sanctified by the blessing of a qualified priest, some had an unclear origin, but were given a priest's blessing. Water of the highest degree was that brought from the Jordan River, the place of Christ's baptism. This water was stored in special vessels, to be used only on rare and important occasions.

Another job the trainees had was related to candles. They were responsible for the perpetual candles, and they were the ones who lit the hundreds of candles that illuminated the church during prayers. Along with the water and candles, the trainees were also responsible for baking the communion bread, which the believers received at the end of mass. They also had to make sure they placed the sweet red wine, made specially for the church, on the altar.

Clergy novices served as the confessional coordinators. St. Michael's, which was a large, central church, had four confessionals, two on each side of the altar. Each booth had two separate entrances, and the only connection between the two was created through the screen, to ensure the confessor's right to complete anonymity. Church leaders made sure that a confessional was available twenty-four hours a day to meet the needs of miners, sailors, night watchmen, or anyone whose sleep was burdened by the gravity of their sins. Therefore, the priests were required to have a permanent shift in the confessionals as part of their scheduled duties and chores. Each shift would be limited to four hours only. A priest would sit in the confessional throughout the shift to receive confessors.

A trainee would be responsible for coordinating and pointing confessors to the next vacant booth. There was no time limit for confession, although there was an understanding of the proper time to be allocated to each confession. When a trainee would notice that a certain confession lasted beyond the usual time, he would knock lightly on the priest's door as a reminder that there are others awaiting his service. At the end of the confession, the trainee would give the priest ten minutes for a breather and then refer the next confessor in line. From midnight, only one confessional would be available.

On Tuesday afternoon, David was preparing to end his shift in the confessional, but before leaving the booth, a new confessor sat across the partition. A familiar scent of perfume tickled his nose. Through the partition he noticed a pair of blue eyes. Unconsciously, his eyes dropped to the marble breasts, but the angle of the partition prevented him from receiving that confirmation.

"Hello, Father."

David immediately recognized the voice, without any need for further confirmation.

"Hello, my child. The good God is listening to you."

"I came to confess before God."

David was excited. The skill and professionalism he acquired over time faded. He discovered that what he thought he had lost forever, had returned in the blink of an eye.

"God's heart is open, his ear is attentive, and he is merciful," he told her, trying to hide his excitement and control his voice, but he was not sure he had succeeded.

"I came to confess before God and tell him that I used to run a brothel."

David regained his composure and his voice stabilized. "The good and benevolent God forgives all sins and iniquities. Bless you and blessed be Mary and may God be with you."

A sigh of relief went through the screen. The blue eyes left the booth.

David wanted to run after her, hug her, feel her breasts, and suck her tongue, but he clung to his seat, knowing that it was not yet time for his shift to end.

***

The next evening, after completing all his duties at the church, David changed into civilian clothes and went down to the market. He passed by the vegetable, fish, and flea markets, and walked to the strange signs district.

The three signs were in place, however, to his surprise, the "**We Won't Sell Betty**" door was open. He peeked inside and discovered that the red foyer had disappeared and that the place had become one big space. He went inside along with other visitors and realized he was in a store laden with groceries. A handsome man in a white shirt and black tie approached him.

"Can I help you, Reverend?"

"Yes," David replied. "Do you sell fish too?"

"No," replied the man politely. "We've realized that we cannot compete with the prices of the fish at the stalls outside."

"I saw a sign outside that you do not sell Betty, so I thought you must be selling fish..."

The short man showed no sign of shame. "Betty is Betty, and fish are fish," he said. "I explained to you why we don't sell fish, but Betty has nothing to do with it. She rented the place to us and insisted that it be put in the contract that we are not allowed to change the name of the place."

A sigh of relief was about to break out of David's chest. Not another brothel. Skilled in controlling his emotions, however, he said to the short man, "Thank you! If so, I'm going to the fish market."

Though he did not go to the fish market, but rather to the promenade. What now? How do I find Betty? Her image did not leave his head. The blue eyes are still piercing, he pondered and walked back to the church.

The following Sunday he was on mass duty. At the end of the ceremony, a lengthy line of worshipers waited to receive the sacramental bread. The basket with the wafers made by the trainee on call was set on a table beside him, and next to it a bottle of blessed wine.

One of the believers, a woman dressed in Sunday clothes and hair covered in a colorful kerchief, waited at a distance in line.

David did not have to guess. He recognized her scent as soon as she entered the church. He took a wafer, brought it to her mouth and blessed her in the name of the Father, the Son, and the Holy Spirit. At the end of the blessing the woman raised her head to thank him of his compassion. Her blue eyes struck him like lightning from the sky. He knew and she knew what they both knew.

She looked down and whispered, "Tomorrow at the boardwalk." She rushed out of the church.

David waited, intoxicated, for the parade of wafers and blessings to end. To him, tomorrow seemed like a week.

Toward noon the next day, David informed the trainee in his service that he was going out for errands and left directly for the promenade.

She was already waiting for him on the bench in the center of the boardwalk, dressed in plain white clothes and a wide-brimmed red hat.

David sat down to her right, as excited as he was all those years ago on the shores of the lake. Betty felt his excitement. She placed her hand on his left arm.

"May I?" she asked awkwardly.

The tongue of the eloquent preacher stuck to the roof of his mouth. He could not say a thing.

"Don't say a word," she said, placing her finger to his lips. "I have come to say goodbye."

"What happened?" he asked in horror.

"I am doing what's good for you and what I have to do."

"What happened?" he asked her again, desperate.

"We're sliding down a slippery slope, and if we don't get a hold of things, it won't be good for either of us."

"I'm willing to take the risk."

"I know," she replied. "But I decided, thanks to you, to change my life and retire to another life, and as strange as it may sound, you are a part of my previous life."

Betty lifted her hat, her face as white as the color of the swans floating in front of them in the river. She kissed him on the lips and walked up the boardwalk without turning her head back.

The church was empty by the afternoon, and so were the confessionals. David entered the confessional on the east side of the church, near the stage, and sat down on the narrow, high chair he knew from the hundreds of confessions his highness had heard.

"I have a lot of thoughts and doubts," he said.

"Do you want to confess or consult?" a voice replied out of the empty side of the confessional.

"Both."

"We're in a confessional, so maybe we should start with a confession?"

"The acquaintance with Betty tore my soul apart. She brought me back to Tamara and my past. I thought I found peace for my mind and soul, but it is not so."

"You have done well, my son," his voice answered

beyond the lattice. "There is nothing better for purifying the soul than the revelation of thought."

"And what is the advice?" David questioned.

"'Many designs are in a man's mind, but it is the Lord's plan that is accomplished' said the wisest man of all."

David wondered if he understood the message, though knocks on the booth's door woke him from his thoughts.

"The time for confession is over," the trainee announced beyond the closed door.

David came out of the booth with his head bowed, knowing that his account with himself was not over yet.

CHAPTER 6 – SHMUEL

Rabbi Nachman had eight daughters. The day his wife Zelda returned from the maternity ward she had told her husband, "No more. We simply do not know how to make boys."

"But…" he responded lamely. "The birth of girls is a sign for boys to come."

"No. We've had eight signs already. Enough is enough," she said impatiently and set off to breastfeed the new baby and tend to her seven older sisters.

Years went by, the girls grew up and the rabbi headed the Moriah Yeshiva in Jerusalem.

The grand yeshiva was a well-known establishment throughout the Land of Israel and among the Jewish Diaspora. Three hundred pupils studied there from infant to scholar before graduation to prepare for their departure on mission to yeshivas, synagogues, and holy sites in Israel and abroad.

Rabbi Nachman was revered by all. Some would whisper that he was a Torah scholar even greater than his father, who founded the yeshiva. Such statements would have previously been considered sacrilegious. He was of high and mighty status attracting hundreds of listeners to his sermons, including some of the great rabbis around.

Once a week a 'day of gathering' was held at the yeshiva, where the rabbi assembled his adult students to bestow his knowledge and wisdom on to them, and to make sure they kept in touch in the future as spiritual leaders of the Torah-keeping world.

The rabbi directed the yeshiva with great skill, wisdom, and common sense. He knew many students personally, and from time to time even attended the Chevruta[3] meetings where they would chat and argue about matters of Torah and wisdom.

Shmuel Meisels attempted to join this yeshiva immediately after his Bar Mitzvah. His admission to the yeshiva was not granted. Fortunately, his mother had a third cousin who traded in textiles in the Old City of Jerusalem. The same cousin would occasionally donate to the yeshiva, and it has already been said by some in the past that there is nothing like a good donation to ensure one passes the entrance exam. And so, a few days after Shmuel's Bar Mitzvah celebration, his father informed him with great pride that he had been accepted to study at the prestigious Moriah yeshiva.

---

3. **Chevruta** is a traditional approach to Talmudic study in which small groups of students analyze, discuss, and debate a shared text.

Early days into his studies, Shmuel proved to be a sharp-witted, bright young man, who devoted all his time to Torah study, and did not deviate his eyes left or right as some of his friends did when the rabbi's daughters turned into women. Once a month Shmuel would spend a weekend off with his family back in the village. On one of these visits, he went for a walk in the fields with his brother, Dudi, who swore him to secrecy before telling him about his girlfriend from the mud village whose eyes were blue, her body copper, and their love golden.

For a split second, a spark of curiosity stirred in Shmuel, however, after Dudi told him that he dreamed of his girlfriend at night, he realized that it was not for him.

"The story about your girlfriend," he told his brother. "Is prohibited to me. On the next visit we will go for a walk, but not to the lake." He recalled the ancient prohibition against visiting the dangerous and now enchanted lake.

From that day on, the two did not discuss matters of the heart, but a tremor of jealousy commanded Shmuel about the degree of freedom his brother possessed.

***

Rabbi Nachman knew of Shmuel's attributes and when his wife, Zelda, reminded him that their daughter, Leah, had come of age, he took action. In the hot summer days, he had notified his wife that he would oblige her request that he take time off from his hard work and spend seven days in the mystic city of Safed, which was known for its Kabbalah studies and cool crisp air.

One hot day, they set out for Safed in an opulent carriage. Before doing so, the rabbi had called Shmuel in to advise him that he would like to stop on their way to Yesodot to visit with his parents privately.

The carriage with Rabbi Nachman and his wife swayed from Jerusalem through Jericho, then north to Tiberius, and after rolling over the rocky road and wiping off much sweat from their brows, they arrived at the home of the rabbi of Yesodot. The driver led the horses to rest and retired himself for a short nap.

The parents sat in the living room of the rabbi's modest home, enjoyed light refreshments prepared by his wife and discussed their business. Shortly after that, Rabbi Nachman and Zelda called for their carriage and headed onward to Safed.

"That's right," said Rabbi Nachman to his wife when they left. "Not everything is perfect, but let us not forget that our Leah is not the most… well, don't forget the leg issue. I am sure that the boy's virtues overcompensate for his brother's misgivings."

The rumbling wheels piercing the village's only street could still be heard when Hannah, in an outpouring of excitement, pounced on her husband.

"Did you hear that?! Rabbi Nachman proposed we'd be his in-laws!"

"But—"

"Oh, stop it with your buts! He even hinted he would absolve you for Dudi's doings!"

"I heard. But did you ask Shmuel if he would agree to this arrangement?"

"Just like you asked him if he would agree to continue his advanced studies at the kollel after he marries—"

"But she is four years his senior!"

"Oh, you are being so petty!"

"That's not petty, it is quite a matter of gravity."

"We raised him to respect his elders. He will do what is right by us and whatever the rabbi asks of him."

"And what does Leah think about this arrangement?"

"On Saturday, two weeks ago, her mother took her to the synagogue for morning prayers and asked her to peek through the curtain onto the men's section…"

"And?"

"She peeked and immediately said yes."

"And how did she know who Shmuel was?" the father asked.

"Before prayers, the rabbi and his wife had agreed that he would seat Shmuel to his right."

"And how do you know all of this?"

"There is talk among women that you men will never

171 AARON BEN SHAHAR

understand. You have too many questions today... all you need to do is remember that next Friday, we will be celebrating with an engagement dinner in Jerusalem during which the couple will first meet."

"Besides," she added. "You should be grateful we won't have to pay a matchmaker."

Rabbi Shlomo and his wife arrived in Jerusalem early. On Thursday, they settled in a small room at the grand Yeshiva headed by one of Rabbi Nachman's old students. On Friday, after evening prayers, they went with Shmuel to the rabbi's apartment located on the Yeshiva's grounds, where they were welcomed in by the rabbi's wife.

Rabbi Nachman was waiting in the living room. He got up and warmly shook their hands. Before Shlomo was able to admire the hundreds of holy books that covered the walls, the rabbi's wife invited them to the table and called her daughter to join.

The table was set for six. The honorable rabbi from Jerusalem sat at the head and facing him was the rabbi from Yesodot. On the one side, Hannah sat with Shmuel by her side while on the other, the rabbi's wife and Leah by her side. The white tablecloth adorned with silver lines was topped with a loaf of braided challah covered with a blue slink cloth with a gold Star of David in its center.

"The cover for the challah bread was passed down to Rabbi Nachman by his great grandmother," Zelda rushed to inform the guests.

A bottle of sweet red wine was placed by the challah. Sabbath candles were lit atop a cabinet laden with holy books.

Rabbi Nachman took his hat off and replaced it with a splendid black yarmulke. He poured wine into the goblets and when he stood up to pour some for Leah, his wife cried out, "Don't give her too much, it's not good for her!"

The rabbi made the blessing and in an unorthodox fashion, congratulated all present by ending the prayer with the words "Mazal Tov."

The first dish served was gefilte fish – minced carp served with a sweet sauce and boiled carrot, with a side of homemade red horseradish. The rabbi broke bread, leaving one small piece of challah for himself and passed the rest on to the guests.

At that moment, Rabbi Shlomo realized that there was no point for his hat, and he replaced it with a white yarmulke he kept in his pocket. He placed his hat on a hanger next to Rabbi Nachman's.

As they finished the appetizers, Leah got up to help her mother clear the plates.

"Don't get up!" her mother cried. "Today, you are like royalty and royals do not clear dishes."

Before that moment, Shmuel had not looked up from his plate and buried his discomfort in the gefilte fish. And now, with Leah, his eyes lifted, and he dared to look at her. She was a tall, slightly heavy, fair-haired girl. When she heard her mother's scolding, she sat down immediately, mortified. Shmuel noticed that her eyes were as soft as Leah's. The other Leah. The next dish was fresh chicken soup and a bowl of toasted croutons.

The Rebbetzin rejected Hannah's offer to help clear the dishes and picked them up herself. Shmuel snuck another look at Leah, but her head was bowed toward the table and her face could not be seen. All he noticed was the dress she was wearing. A white Sabbath dress with a starched collar that covered her neck entirely, and sleeves longer than her arms.

The main course was roasted chicken that was kept heated on the Sabbath hotplate placed on the kitchen counter. Side dishes of rice and sweet glazed carrots with raisins were in the center of the table.

Shmuel, who wore a white shirt he bought especially for the occasion and old black pants, made his best effort not to get the thick gravy on his clothes or on his beard that was black as the olives that Jamila from the village of Fajar sold in the market near Rosh Pina.

For dessert, the rabbi's wife served compote with dried figs, apples, prunes, and raisins.

"The raisins are from Hebron," she said. "They are the best, by far."

While serving dessert, Hannah looked at the hostess' dress, a long pink dress that blurred the contour of her plump body. Fortunately, I chose my mother's dress rather than the one narrow dress at the waist – it would have shamed the Rebbetzin, she said to herself, quite chuffed.

"My grandmother also used to make compote like this," she contributed to the conversation. "Though the raisins were from Wlodawa."

"What is Wlodawa?" Zelda asked.

"It is a town in Poland, where my parents came from. People there tried to grow grapes, however, because of the cold, the grapes never fully ripened so they made them into raisins."

"Ha!" was Zelda's riled up response.

At the end of the meal, the rabbi spoke about this week's Torah portion. The guests heard the long sermon but did not listen. Rabbi Nachman then invited his guest to say the prayer after the meal and as soon as he had finished, Hannah turned to her bag hanging on the back of her chair and took out a book.

"This is our engagement gift," she said to a mortified Leah. "This is a Tzena Urena[4] book that has been passed down and around the women in our family for many years. I now hand it to you with great joy and pride."

Leah took the book with a feeble hand. Rabbi Nachman and Rebbetzin Zelda whispered between them, embarrassed.

Then the rabbi rose, went to the next room, and soon returned with a black cap as those given to the yeshiva graduates, and handed the gift to his guest.

"May God bless you with many sons," he said and sat down proudly in his chair.

It was time to say goodbye. Shmuel shook the rabbi's hand unconvincingly, nodded his head goodbye to the rabbi's wife, and made no effort to meet Leah's eyes.

That night he had trouble sleeping, and the next day he rushed to the synagogue to spend his day praying and reading the Torah. He had avoided making eye contact with Rabbi Nachman all day. That evening, after the evening prayers, he parted with his parents who were

---

4. **Tzena Urena** written by Jacob ben Isaac Ashkenazi (1550-1625) of Janów Lubelski (near Lublin, Poland), the book is sometimes called the Women's Bible. It is a Yiddish-language prose work structured in conjunction with the weekly Torah portions and mixes Biblical passages with teachings from Judaism's Oral Torah such as the Talmud and others.

about to head back to the village at dawn and explained to them that he was tired and wanted to go to bed early.

"Do you see how excited the boy is?" Hannah said to her husband. "The truth is, I'm just as excited."

***

The next days were difficult for Shmuel. He had a hard time being at the yeshiva as his head felt dizzy and his soul was uneasy. For days, he would walk the narrow streets of the old city of Jerusalem, feeling the walls closing in on him and threatening to collapse and bury him under the rubble.

One day, his feet took him the Mount of Olives. After wandering among the old graves, he sat on one facing west toward the old city of Jerusalem. He suddenly burst into cries like never before. Tears rolled down his beard, wetting his shirt and his dusty trousers.

His whole life flushed through his tears – a life of capitulation, submission, and greyness. His consent was never required for anything that happened in his life. From birth, through circumcision to the kindergarten where he was kept with lots of other babies, howling and wetting themselves. When he was six years old, his mother enrolled him in the village Cheider.

Every morning, after reciting the Modeh Ani[5] prayer, the teacher walked between the rows of students, instructed them to clench their fingers, only to then strike their fingertips with a ruler.

"If they deserve it – good. And if not, it will serve as payment for something in the future." That was the teacher's pedagogical notion. The students accepted the beatings with conformity and humility and continued the morning prayer in which they thanked God for returning their souls to them, depositing them to him at night. And after receiving the deposit, why would they complain about their teacher?

Soon after his Bar Mitzvah, Shmuel transferred to a yeshiva where he invested all his energy and talents. He endeavored to please the teachers and the rabbi of the Yeshiva, expecting recognition and perhaps even gratitude of some sort. His daily schedule was set, adjusted to fit the times of the prayers, and included many prohibitions and restrictions dictated by the heads of the yeshiva. Clothes, food, Chevruta meetings, and other activities were conducted under the strict rules.

Shmuel also shed tears over his life in his own home; for his mother he loved so much, who dominated his life with

---

5. **Modeh Ani** is a prayer recited upon waking up, thanking God for renewing, and restoring one's soul each morning.

love, and over his father who he had admired so much and would do his best to please and make up for the dreams he did not fulfill himself.

And now I am expected to marry someone I cannot look at neither in the day nor the night, he thought sadly. The lump in his throat dissolved and closure was found. The sun had set in the west, the city lights came on, his tears had all dried and he returned upright and vigorous to the yeshiva.

On the weekend he arrived at his parents' house in the village. After a short rest, he turned to his brother's wardrobe, which he had never opened, took out his shorts and shirt, which were a little too big for his size, and headed for the lake.

Shmuel had never been to the lake because of his mother's warnings that the mud might cause one to drown, and that village children would get abducted around that area. During days off from Yeshiva, he heard in amazement about Dudi's visits to the lake and was astounded that he had not yet drowned or even been abducted.

He went through the reeds that his brother had told him about and looked for the piggy trail. Then all of a sudden, just like in a fairy tale, right next to him came out of the undergrowth a pig. She waved hello with her short tail and disappeared on to the other side of the path followed by five little piglets.

Shmuel was so surprised by the piglets that he forgot to spit three times in four directions as required and as a mitzvah when encountering an unclean animal. After the last of the piglets disappeared, his legs led him to the huge oak tree that grew on the shores of the lake. He sat down on a stump of the tree trunk and it felt like he had been sitting on it forever.

So spectacularly serene.

On the western side of the lake stretched the Golan Heights, bluish, greenish, near but far. The lake at its foot was peaceful and dormant. A flock of cranes danced in the water and pelicans aired their broad beaks. The kingfisher, known to him from his brother's stories, stood on a branch gliding above the water, and the shadow it cast attracted a school of gullible fish. Shmuel was flooded with longing. Yearning for love, for his prodigal brother, and for a life he never had.

Knowing about his brother's conversion did not affect his feelings towards him. It did not even come as a surprise. Dudi was the type to choose for himself, he thought. These yearnings were so tangible and heavy that he could feel them in his hands. It was a longing for everything he had not known in his life – freedom, openness, passion, dreams, and for the liberty to choose love.

All of Dudi's stories unfolded before him, as if they had shared that little spot. Stories about reed and Cyperus, sky and sea, mountains near and far, white donkeys, blue eyes, and a body the color of copper. He sank into a caressing nap and a warm dream, wondering what Dudi would do in his stead.

The cranes gathered for their night's sleep, the pelicans were quiet, the kingfisher took off from the branch and flew to his wife with his belly full of little fish, and Shmuel felt it was time he returned to the village.

Friday night dinner in the small house in the village with his parents and his beautiful younger sister, Esther, felt very pleasant for him. The four of them spent a peaceful evening together at the end of which Esther retired to see her friends, and his parents invited him to sip tea with them on the terrace.

The atmosphere there, however, was different. Shmuel felt the distress that descended upon his parents. The chatter and joy during dinner was replaced by silence and sadness. Shmuel looked astonished at his father, who was bowed in silence and noticed that his mother was about to burst into tears.

"Did something happen?"

"Yes!" his mother said. "We must talk to you about a painful subject." Her voice cracked.

Shmuel was horrified. "Is it a serious illness? Esther?"

"Dudi," his mother's lips whispered.

He was shocked to hear the name that was taboo in that house. From the very day his father tore his shirt in mourning over the son he had lost, his name was banned.

"You know how happy and proud we are to see you start a family with a righteous woman from house of great Torah scholars, fulfilling all of our hopes and dreams. Know that we have never forgotten about Dudi," she said with a tremor in her voice and tears in her eyes.

"Neither have I. But what would you have me do?"

"We are asking that you go to England and bring Dudi back to us. We are sure you would be able to convince him to return to his faith and family."

"And what about my studies? And the engagement?"

"The Mitzvah of 'and your children shall return to their own border' trumps studying," his mother replied while his father nodded in agreement. "There is some time until the wedding. Think how wonderful it would be to see Dudi dancing at your wedding."

Shmuel's heart rejoiced. He'd spent all of these years dreaming of seeing his brother again and hearing from him face-to-face about his motives to convert and his life as a Christian priest.

"As you wish!" he said.

***

Shmuel was privileged to christen the new 'Diligence' line to Beirut. Led by a pair of horses, the six-seater carriage left Tiberias, passed through Rosh Pina, crossed Metula, and made a brief stop at Marjayoun to rest and water the horses. From there on to the coast up to Beirut. A quick calculation made him realize that the ticket on the new line is a whole pound cheaper than a ticket on the old line from Rosh Pina to the port of Beirut via Haifa, not to mention the time it saves – two hours on a rocky road.

He arrived late to Beirut. He dined at the only restaurant on the city's beautiful promenade to receive a kosher certificate from the chief rabbinate there. Shmuel slept in one of the two bedrooms set up on the roof of the restaurant by Richie, the owner.

The next day he went down to the restaurant, took the kosher food package Richie had prepared for him for the five-day voyage, and walked the short walk to the port. The "Queen Mary" steamship already had smoke in its funnels. In its advertisement, the travel company undertook the following: "The new 'Queen Mary' steamer is a fast ship that transports passengers from the port of Beirut to the port of London in just five days. Payment is thirty-nine pounds each way, not including meals. Children under one year travel for free."

Below the caption, the company added an image of the ship with its two sleek funnels and white smoke curling out of them.

On the deck of the ship, Shmuel met a tall sailor who examined the ticket he was holding and asked him to come with him. The sailor led Shmuel to an endless staircase in the middle of the ship. Finally, he pointed to a cubicle located in a row of tiny rooms below the waterline and above the engine rooms of the ship. In his small cabin, Shmuel found a bunk bed that took up most of the space.

Shmuel barely had time to put his backpack and food package under the bed before the room shook violently. The ship's engines were turned on, the noise was so loud that he had to flee the little cabin for as long as he could and went up the spiral staircase to the deck. The horns of the ship leaving the port sounded like the pleasing chanting of the yeshiva children's choir.

At night, when the lights of Beirut dissipated and fatigue took over, Shmuel dragged himself into the cabin. His tiredness was great, and he fell asleep, as the loud noise from above, balanced that which came from below. He sat down on the bed, his head bowed, careful not to hit the top bunk. When he checked the source of the noise, he discovered to his astonishment that at the top of the bunk bed was a man whose dimensions exceeded the width of the bed and whose snoring matched that of the ship's engines.

Shmuel ejected himself away from the 'noise sandwich' straight to the deck and spent the night, as well as the next few there, on a discarded sail. He had many hours to look at the stars at night and loads of questions. Does he really want Dudi back? And if so, why? And what about himself?

He divided the food package he had bought from Richie before the voyage for five days, yet it was only enough for four. On Thursday, Shmuel sat on the deck and stared hungrily at a passenger who took a huge bite of a thick sandwich. When the passenger noticed his gaze, he approached him and offered to share the sandwich. Shmuel in his hunger accepted the offer, and when he finished eating, he found that he had eaten a foreign sandwich without a kosher certificate and to his surprise the sky did not fall, and the ship did not sink.

The ship did not sail to London as promised in the advertisement, but rather to the port of Southampton, where he boarded a train to London. Dudi was waiting for him on the train platform. The two fell into each other's arms.

Dudi passed on wearing the clerical outfit but not the cross necklace he wore on his chest, and Shmuel with his overgrown beard wore trousers and a coat of the same color as well as an elaborate black hat, the kind great students would wear on joyous occasions.

The hug went on and on, conveying a message of deep longing, and when they broke away from each other Dudi's first words were, "How are Dad and Mom?"

"They are both fine, I think, but they miss you terribly."

"And what about Esther?"

"Growing up."

"How I miss them..." Dudi said with teary eyes.

After a few minutes of silence, Dudi picked up Shmuel's light baggage despite his dismay, and said, "Come with me!"

Not far from the port was a hostel run by the Anglican Church and intended for pilgrims. They took a key from the doorman to a simple yet comfortable room that Dudi had booked in advance and went into the room.

"We have a lot to talk about," Shmuel said. "But I haven't slept in five nights, and I am absolutely shattered..."

Before he could hear his brother's reaction, he collapsed onto the bed and fell asleep.

Dudi, however, could not sleep. The longing for his family was a constant part of his daily life and did not stop for a moment. The severance imposed by his father tore his soul apart, and Shmuel's presence amplified the pain.

The news of his brother's visit came as a surprise. From his acquaintance with the people involved, he knew that Shmuel was not one for surprises. He had always admired his brother's self-discipline and ability to live with reality in peace. There was no way Shmuel would suddenly decide to leave the yeshiva, even for a short time, just to visit his brother or to see the "Big Ben" in person... he thought amusedly.

Shmuel fell asleep in his black coat, and luckily for the hat, it was thrown to the floor on his way to bed.

Dudi gently peeled the coat off his brother's body, placing it on a chair. He put the hat on the coat. I'm so glad you're here, he told Shmuel silently. You bring me the scents of home. It's almost like seeing Dad and Mom... He covered him with a blanket, parted ways with his own insomnia and woke up in the morning ready for a brand-new day.

Shmuel was still asleep.

After twelve hours of sleep, Shmuel woke up, washed his hands and face, and did not utter a single word as it would be prohibited to speak before prayer. He pulled his prayer bag out of the suitcase and out of it, a tallit.[6] He draped it

---

6. Tallit is a Jewish prayer shawl worn over clothes during prayers.

on his body and wrapped a tefillin[7] on his forehead and left arm. After the morning prayer he greeted his brother with a good morning hug.

The modest room did not even offer a cup of coffee. The two left the hostel and headed toward the nearby river Thames. Pubs and cafes on the promenade were inviting, however, Shmuel refused to go into any of them as they did not have a Kosher stamp. With their bellies rumbling and dry mouths, they kept on marching upriver in search of a Kosher place.

Their knees were getting tired when Dudi noticed a small grocery store. He seated Shmuel on a bench between the shop and the river and came back after about a quarter of an hour with a cup of coffee and cheese toast for himself, and a paper cup with tea and plain toast for his brother.

"They don't sell meat," he tried to reassure his brother.

The hunger subdued Shmuel. He grabbed the toast and chewed quickly, looking left and right not to be caught in his spoilage by an observant Jew by chance. The view was spectacular, and the two spent the day walking down the streets of London. Shmuel took in the landscapes, the sights, and the people. I'll talk to him tomorrow, he

---

7. Tefillin is a set of small black leather boxes with leather straps containing scrolls of parchment inscribed with verses from the Torah.

thought, not forgetting for a moment the purpose of his trip.

The next day, as planned, they took the train to Newcastle. The journey was long, and they arrived at Dudi's house only in the evening. Tomorrow is a new day and anyway Dudi invited me for three days, my mission can wait, he thought.

Tired but happy, they each headed to their room in the small yet pleasant apartment that the church allocated for their vicar. Shmuel appreciated his brother's consideration, who made sure to remove the cross above the bed and leave only that which hung above his own bed. Even with the cross gone, he could not sleep. Thoughts and reflections raced through his mind and scarred his soul.

The torment he thought would not befall him from the moment he boarded the ship in Haifa, had now come back tenfold. All the prohibitions, restrictions, demands, instructions, and commandments that persecuted him in his studies, at home, and everywhere in his life, all stood before him in a row.

My younger brother, Dudi, spends his days free and happy, and the cross he wears on his chest is also an act of choice, while I continue to run in a rigid box that dictates everything in my entire life. The dawn that refused to come finally surrendered to nature's laws and spread its light. Shmuel left his room and was surprised to find his brother sitting in the small kitchen corner.

"Good morning," said Shmuel, anxious when he realized that he had broken the prohibition of speech before the morning prayer.

He then prayed and when he finished, he folded the tallit, rolled the tefillin, and sat with his brother at the table. On the table he found a jug of tea, a plate of hot toast, poached eggs, and slices of pale vegetables that never got enough sun. Shmuel welcomed the tea his brother had poured for him and placed on the plate in front of him fresh and hot toast, one egg, and chopped vegetables.

"Bon appetit," he said to Dudi and began to eat the humble breakfast.

He drank the tea completely astound by the fact that he was eating in a Christian's house and not just a Christian – a priest, without checking if the food and dishes were kosher.

Dudi poured him some more of the quenching tea and said, "Would you like to come to work with me?"

Of course, he thought. It would be a great opportunity to find quality time with him throughout the day and talk to him man-to-man, brother-to-brother.

The church was only steps away from the house. Shmuel sat awkwardly on the last bench in the church, close to the exit door. Dudi went to the tiny side room by the entrance and came out of it as David, dressed in proper priests clothing. He walked from the entrance through rows of pews to the stage in front and nodded his head at the congregation.

Shmuel was surprised to see them all bowing their heads in reverence to greet his younger brother.

After inspecting the small, elegant church, he examined the crowd. In the middle of the front row sat three elderly ladies who listened attentively to the sermon his brother had begun to deliver and nodded steadily. In the second row to the right sat a man in his forties in a tartan jacket and a flat cap. His fingers drummed on his knee nervously and it was obvious that he was waiting for the sermon to end. In the same row sat a lady in a festive white dress and a matching headscarf. She was holding a five-year-old boy tightly, who seemed to be unimpressed by the vicar's statements and all he had wanted was to escape to the nearby playground.

At the end of the sermon, the three elderly ladies, the man, and the woman in white, dragged the child to the stage. David stood and to Shmuel's amazement, placed in the mouths of the each in turn, what seemed to him from a distance like a tough cake like those his mother would bake during Passover.

As the man passed by David, he whispered something to his ear, and David leaned toward him, nodding his head in agreement.

After the four women left the church, Shmuel saw the man go up to a cubicle he had never noticed until that very moment. David came down from the stage and entered the same cubicle from another entrance. Long minutes went by, and Shmuel sat bored in the back bench until he saw the man coming out of the confessional with great excitement, holding his hat in his hand, revealing a large bald patch on his head.

Shmuel waited curiously for his brother, until he saw him come out of the room and go to the tiny side room, where he took off his clerical outfit. Dudi returned.

"Sorry," said Dudi. "But you did want to see where I work. Now we may have our time."

He led him to a small, modest chapel adjacent to the main space of the church. It had three comfortable armchairs around a dark, wooden table with a jug of water placed on it. They sat in silence, a little embarrassed by the situation.

"Did you want to tell me something?" Dudi broke the silence.

"Yes," Shmuel replied, stuttering, and debating how to present things to his brother. He gulped and found his courage. "Your conversion to Christianity as I saw it today is very impressive. I saw your face glowing; I saw the excitement in the people, but you never told me why you really converted to Christianity. I know you sent a letter to Mother, but she never told us what was in it."

Rain began to drizzle outside. It was cool in the chapel, but Dudi's body was not trembling because of the cold. He found it difficult to speak. A few minutes later, he raised his head and turned to his brother. "I converted to Christianity to save my life," he replied with a face white as a sheet. He grabbed Shmuel's hand in one, and a glass of water in the other, bringing it close to his mouth. Shmuel feared that his brother would faint.

"Never mind; no need," he cried out in concern for his brother's health. "You don't have to answer me."

His fingers that gripped his brother's hand turned white and the intensity was now causing it to hurt. "No, no," Dudi responded, wanting to finally unload the burden of all those years. "I actually do want to talk."

He took another sip of the water, looked straight at him, and let go of his hand.

Shmuel waited in silence and wonder, and Dudi began to speak as if to himself.

"My conversion to Christianity has nothing to do with religion. Anyone who tells you that they suddenly had some sort of epiphany and decided to convert to Christianity or Islam – just don't believe them. I was faced with two choices. I chose the second, easier choice, and you probably understand now what the first choice would have been."

Shmuel's body shrank. His head dropped to the table and his mind was anxious about what was to come.

After lengthy seconds went by, Dudi stopped quivering and kept talking to his brother, or perhaps to himself.

"I am a traitor. I betrayed two good people to their deaths." He burst into tears in a bitter cry.

The minutes passed and a horrified Shmuel kept silent.

Dudi collected himself and said, "On that awful and rushed day the Turks wanted to take Dad and hang him in the main square of Damascus. You were in Jerusalem, and I was with myself, and my own destiny and I came to a decision. I gave the Turks the addresses of two wanted men, so they wouldn't take Dad. I later saw in the newspaper the photograph of their bodies swinging on the gallows in the main square of Damascus.

"That morning, despair had ended my life as I knew it, and so I decided to commit suicide. I took the bed sheet from my room at the hostel, tied it to the window and wrapped it around my neck. But then a miracle happened. The bells of the nearby church rang. A soft, obscure hand pulled me from the abysses of despair. To the church.

"I was welcomed there with love and no questions asked. They managed to contain my pain and restore my soul. My whole conversion process was a result of timing and coincidence. If there had been a Buddhist monastery or a Zen temple in the building next door, you would be seeing a different Dudi. But there was a church there.

"The pastor in that church saved my life. He opened the door for me, and I rushed in through it. He revealed to me another faith that spread its arms toward me. Christianity was for me a lifeline that I clung to in order to get out of my life crisis.

"There. Now you know why and how I became a Christian."

"And what about Judaism?" Shmuel asked.

"Judaism is a part of me," Dudi replied. "I feel like a borrowed Jew, and I know and want that when my time comes, I will be buried as a Jew."

Darkness fell and the rain got stronger. The two walked to the house, sipped tea in silence, and each went to his own room.

"Your train to London leaves tomorrow," Dudi reminded his brother.

A sleepless night passed over Shmuel. Dudi saved his life, he thought to himself, but what about my soul?

The next morning the teapot was waiting on the table in its usual place. Shmuel gave up the morning prayer and said to his brother, "I want to come with you to church."

This time he sat in the third row, while the three elderly ladies sat in the middle of the front row. Had he not seen them leave church yesterday, he would have sworn they had not moved since then. The man and woman with the child were not there. In the third row he saw a young couple holding hands and gulping up the words of the sermon delivered by the priest, who was so beknown to him.

When the sermon had ended, the five attendees turned to the stage and received the holy wafer. Upon leaving the alter, Shmuel stopped Dudi on his way to the small side room to change his clothes.

"I want to make a confession," he said to Dudi's astonishment.

"Why would you want to make a confession?"

"You said that in your church, anyone can make a confession regardless of their religion or faith."

"True," replied Dudi. "But I am your brother. If you have something to say to me, why not sit outside with me? It won't rain today."

"I'm scared," said Shmuel. "I worry that in an open conversation between us, I won't fully have the courage to say what's in my heart. I am also afraid that you won't be able to truly accept what I have to say."

The dark circles around Dudi's eyes from lack of sleep the night before, deepened. Anxiety gripped his throat. They walked to the confessional.

Through the lattice, Dudi saw his brother's aching eyes and thought of the hundreds of confessions he had heard, most of which ended with the comforting statement, " I absolve you from your sins in the name of the Father and of the Son and of the Holy Spirit."

But what does Shmuel want to confess? What was his sin? What does he have to do with the Holy Trinity? The familiar confessional and tight priest's collar brought him back to his senses. A first rule in confession theory, Dudi recalled his first lesson in Christian college, is to sever any personal ties with the confessor. And the second rule is to give the confessor the feeling that the whole world is attentive to them.

He addressed the confessor in a sympathetic voice, "How can I help you, my son?"

"I want to convert to Christianity," was the response.

***

The third rule is to maintain maximum self-discipline and restraint and pay equal attention to a serial killer or old woman, who took a double dose of communion, Dudi remembered but failed miserably in adhering to it.

Upon hearing his brother's statement, he lost his temper, the peace of mind, the openness expected of him, and the understanding of others. As a confessor he had already faced long silences, mental anguish, torment, and mental crises, but he did not face such a test. All his studies and experience did not help him deal with such a heartbreaking statement made by his brother, his own flesh.

Long minutes of shock and silence lingered between the two, and at last Dudi mustered the courage and turned to his brother beyond the lattice. "Let's go outside."

The two left the confessionals to the nearby chapel and sat facing each other.

"I took you to see my workplace, not to get ideas."

"Don't flatter yourself," Shmuel replied cynically. "I didn't get enlightened because of you and Jesus didn't appear before me in a dream. I learned from someone sitting in front of me that conversion is rooted in a mental crisis, and that is where I'm coming from."

Dudi was speechless.

"I had a question and you answered it," said Shmuel. "And you have a question you won't ask, but I will answer it: Yes, my dear brother, my confessing pastor, I am in a deep existential crisis. I have run out of inhibitions, and I want you to hold my hand."

The two brothers sat silent, hand-in-hand, in an intimate closeness like they had never felt before.

"I've had enough of my life," said Shmuel. "I've had enough of my life as it is now. I feel like a picture in a frame. I've been framed. I can't just step out of it, and I can't even choose its color. Other people decide when and where to hand it.

"I mustn't think, mustn't dream, and I mustn't sin. You once told me about Tamara, your friend from the mud village and I didn't want to listen to you. 'That's my brother's punishment,' I told myself. 'That's what you get when you think of blue-eyed girlfriends instead of 'Recite it day and night.' But the truth is that ever since that meeting, I haven't stopped being envious of you. I was jealous of your freedom to choose and your ability to decide what and who to love… very quickly, I realized how much I needed my own 'Tamara,' and I wouldn't have cared if her eyes were brown…

"My crisis became existential when the parents I love so much decided with other parents who would be my wife. Do you understand? They interfered with my love, my freedom of choice, the very basic foundations of my life. They decided I would father children who are not love children. So, I decided. I am not ready to continue in such a life, my new life will not be put into frames by others, and I will not be hung by nails.

"I thought I had the ability to make the change within the framework of my life and find a solution to my troubled soul, but I quickly concluded that I have not the mental strength needed for it and that I must choose between a purposeless life and another life. But believe me, the choice before me is no less difficult. I have always envied you for your decision-making ability and your determination. I never believed I would be like you, but I've had enough. It is a matter of it's now or never and I've made my decision."

The two sat exhausted and emptied. The sun cleared the fog, and the chirping of birds filled the air. Shmuel stared piercingly at his brother.

"I know you love me," he told him. "And I know you see in me your wise older brother. And I also know what's going through your head now. So, let me tell you a story. One day, after much deliberation, I gathered my courage and said to our beloved mother: 'I never understood why you sent me to study in the Cheider while you sent Dudi to study in a regular school.' Mother looked at me for a long time and replied, 'Not everything needs to be understood, and not everything can be understood.'

"I did not understand the answer then, but I do understand it now. You will never tell me, but I know what you think. My brother's motivation to convert to Christianity, you say to yourself, is not clear. Is it because of one Leah, one teacher, and one inadequate life system one would change their religion?

"So, this is it, my brother. Not everything needs to be understood and not everything can be understood. You are a rebel, and I am a runaway. I do not know how to resist, nor do I know how to commit suicide, but I do know how to escape, and this is my escape before I sink into a life of nothing but suicidal thoughts."

Shmuel's shoulders rose, his eyes twinkled, and a load of years fell over his stooped back. A tear rolled down Dudi's left eye. He stroked his brother's head and said softly, "You will be late for the train, but if it is your decision, I will give you an address to which you can turn to in London."

"Yes," he replied. "And I also know what to do."

At the train station, the two embraced tightly and let their tears fall. Shmuel knew where he would live in London and the location of the Anglican church. He signed up for an introduction to Christianity course and informed the priest who interviewed him that he would like to join Seminary to study theology. Before the course had started, he collected all the strength he had in him to send his parents a brief telegram:

Do not expect me to return any time soon. I have decided to follow my brother's footsteps, to convert and become a priest.

I love you dearly,
Shmuel.

***

With hunched shoulders and hazy eyes, the village rabbi sat in front of the committee members, who were astonished to see that right in front of their eyes, white hairs were appearing on his beard, and that seemingly out of nowhere, old age was coming over him. The silence was heavy, and the tension was high.

"What happened?" Shaul the dairy farmer asked.

The rabbi swallowed and could not make a sound.

"Did the fever plague anyone in your family?" asked Fischel, who was at the time responsible for the village's perfume manufacturing operation.

The rabbi's tongue clung to the roof of his mouth and refused to let go.

"Maybe we should call the doctor?" suggested Abram, who was always the worrier. "I think he is having a heart attack."

"Something... worse," the rabbi managed to say.

"What could be worse than a fever, a heart attack, or a disease?" the committee member declared.

"My two sons have converted to Christianity," the rabbi groaned and collapsed unconscious on the floor.

CHAPTER 7 – ESTHER

Esther was a godsend: her hair was yellow like hay, her face was white like almond blossoms, her eyes were blue as the sky on a bright spring day, and her lips were the color of the cherry that ripened at the foot of Mount Hermon. A mischievous girl, dancing and bouncing like a flock of cranes, loved, and revered by her friends. Until Dudi left the village.

The departure of the venerated brother, her partner in mischief, who served as a safe place for her to escape to from the rigid demands at home and at school, made it difficult for her. She accepted his conversion to Christianity with a hint of curiosity. She always knew that Dudi was at his core rebellious and possessed the need to search for the other.

She respected the Jewish tradition she absorbed at home and set the guidelines for her life. She studied in religious schools, and her social network came from the same traditional circles, but the boycott imposed on Dudi after his conversion to Christianity did not suit her. As a devoted and educated daughter she obeyed her father's instructions not to make any contact with Dudi, however, deep inside she knew that if she would meet him, she would be the first to pounce on him in a loving embrace.

"You know, Esther's brother is a priest," she heard one close friend whisper to a mutual friend at the Sabbath reception.

For the first time she realized that beyond the family crisis, Dudi's conversion would have an impact on her social life as well. And as if that were not enough, Shmuel also converted to Christianity. His conversion was by then a real wreckage in the family.

Her father lost years right before her eyes, and her mother buried herself under deep depression. But the social rift was no less profound. On girls' night, the chair next to her was always empty, and in any case, she did not partake in the whispers in which most of them would engage.

The great family crisis deepened on the day her mother asked her, "Aren't you going to Rebecca's wedding today?"

Rebecca, her best friend, and confidant, with whom she had shared a bench at school for many years, was getting married. Not only did she not share the news with Esther, but she did not even invite her to her wedding either. The web of silence around her grew stronger. She felt the glances from behind her and noticed all the eyes that had been diverted from her now in front of her.

One of the girls, who one day noticed her painful gaze, pulled her aside in a moment of charity and whispered to her secretly, "It's all because of your brothers."

***

The weeping willow bowed its head, rounded and wailing. Its branches bowed as if carrying on their backs a burden of suffering and mourning. Its elongated leaves bowed to the ground, tears falling from their sharp ends.

Tears also flowed from Esther's eyes and soaked the pillow where she had buried her head.

"How did this happen to me again?"

Only a few minutes had passed since Ephraim the matchmaker informed her that Moti had changed his mind. Not that Moti was to her as fragrant as a spring day or as beautiful as drops of dew in the morning… he was simply the default.

"Asther," Ephraim said. "I give up."

Ephraim, the super-matchmaker, made a name for himself as a pairer of pairs and connector of connections far and wide. His reputation was known all over the Land of Israel, and his long hand plucked brides and grooms from as far away as London, and even New York.

"We shall find a groom for Esther as well," he assured her worried parents, but his efforts were in vain.

"I cannot overcome the problem," he told Esther and her parents at a late meeting over a steaming cup of tea.

After the meeting Esther informed her parents that she was going to skip dinner and went for a night walk through the streets of the village. When she returned, she went to her room, and before putting on her nightgown, stood naked in front of the mirror. She was absolutely beautiful. Her breasts firm, her belly flat, her neck long. The linen hair she had as a child had turned into blond locks that fell down her shoulders, and the years were kind to her blue eyes that widened and deepened. When she walked around the village, no one could remain indifferent.

These were mixed glances of admiration, envy, gloat, and much pity. 'It won't do her much good,' said the looks.

However, before the meeting with Ephraim when he would admit defeat, he came to her house in a shiny black cape and a matching cap on his head, and his black beard neatly groomed.

"I have scheduled a meeting for you with Moti," he told Esther.

She did not know Moti, but her worried parents knew his family. His father was a tinsmith in the nearby town of Rosh Pina, and connoisseurs said he was not among the best in his profession. One time, he attached a left shoe to a horse's right hoof. The horse and rider stumbled and got hurt. The tinsmith went to court presided by Esther's father, who ordered the rider to pay compensation in the amount of ten Bishliks.

Esther and Moti met in the plaza and went for a walk to the lake, where they told each other about themselves. Moti proudly told her that his father had promised him that one day he would take over his business. Before the end of the walk, under Ephraim's guidance, Moti gave her a kiss on the cheek, and the two arranged to meet again in the future.

But there was no future as Moti had second thoughts.

"What happened?" Esther asked Ephraim doubtlessly disappointed or perhaps happy that she had escaped the arrangement.

"His parents object."

"Why?"

Ephraim bowed his head. He did not know how to talk to the rabbi's beautiful daughter, but in the end, gathered courage.

"They do not want their grandchildren's uncles to be Christian priests, knowing that Moti was impressionable..."

The famous matchmaker left the rani's house defeated. With his head bowed he thought of his wife's words and murmured into his beard, "Bluma was right, water will never come out of this rock."

***

For many years, Esther worked as a sewing teacher at the "Bnot Yaakov" religious school for girls. The days of World War II did not agree with her. Detached from her two priestly brothers, she lived with her parents in a small apartment. As she walked the village streets, she was followed by the gossip about the rabbi's daughter being left without brothers and without a match.

The craft of sewing, which she once saw as a vocation, had also eroded in her mind. The needle eye and the thread that once filled her life were dwarfed to a size that fit their dimensions. One evening, while flipping through a newspaper and reading about the Allies' victories over the Nazis, she noticed at the bottom of the inside page of an ad that the "NAAFI" fashion outlet was looking for workers for the chain's stores in Palestine.

"NAAFI" was a chain of convenience stores set up by the British government to cater to the families of soldiers who served in the British Army. During World War II, the chain expanded to employ thirty-five thousand workers. Its branches were opened anywhere British soldiers served or where their families lived, anywhere in the world.

The chain offered a wide variety of products at affordable prices, including products that could not be obtained during the war in the open market. Some of the families received free vouchers as well as basic products for free.

The job offer suited her and the change was something that she needed. She submitted her application to the address in the ad, and to her astonishment was invited for an interview in a gray office building in downtown Haifa. A week later, she was surprised once again when she received a message that she had been hired.

"My name is George, but you can call me King." the store manager, in Bermuda trousers and socks pulled up to the knee introduced himself to the new employee, giggling pleased with himself.

"My name is Esther, but you can call me Elizabeth," she replied in her modest, long-sleeved dress. Her answer reinforced the laughter that washed over him.

"No problem," he replied. "You will call me Joe and I will call you Eti, I don't remember your name anyway. What did you say your name was?"

"Okay," Esther agreed, surprised by the immediate fondness forged between them.

"But don't tell your husband. Husbands don't like their wives giving their bosses nicknames..."

"Don't worry, I have no one to tell."

After the exchange of smiles, George introduced her to rest of the staff. Apart from him, there was an English cashier, a faded and sour-faced woman, two maintenance workers, and her, sales worker – Esther.

"A lot of people were interested in the job," he told her in his small office, which was located in front of the store entrance. "We preferred you for a few reasons. We were looking for a woman of the right age and handsome appearance." He winked at her with his left eye. "And it was important to us that you speak Hebrew, even if it is an English chain. There are many Jewish families in Haifa whose men serve in the British Army, most of them in Egypt, and the army helps these families with basic groceries for free and significant discounts on various products. It is important for the army that they feel like the army is not abandoning them. I think if you improve your English a little bit, you will be a perfect seller, and your funny Palestinian accent will only help sales."

George, or Joe, as she had gotten used to calling him, was to her liking from the moment they first met. Tall, reddish hair, blue eyes, and the manners of an English gentleman, all made him different from the men she met in the village. His rolling laughter would infect her too, a welcome change after years of sadness, disappointment, and frustration. His Hebrew also made her laugh. He was quite the chatterbox, and already in the first hour of their meeting he told her that he worked in the Palestine department of the British Colonial Office in London, and that as part of his job he was sent to attend a course in Hebrew. At one point he moved to the Palestine branch at the King David Hotel in Jerusalem, and after feeling he had done his share there, was happy to accept the offer to serve as the manager of the NAAFI store in Haifa.

"Now that we know that I'm the manager and you the saleswoman, let me introduce you to the shop," he told her in Hebrew with his English accent.

The store was amazing. There were no shops in the village of Yesodot. Identical houses with white walls and red roofs stood on both sides of the main street. Behind each house was a plot of land, with beds of vegetables for self-consumption as well as a barn with one cow and sometimes two, which provided milk for drinking and for making homemade cheese. Vibrant chickens roamed every yard and lay free-range eggs.

There were also public plots where residents tried to make a living, such as growing roses for perfume production, or strawberry bushes for the silk industry.

The two commercial units operating in the village were Hannah's dairy farm, preceded by Weinschel's bakery. Old Weinschel was a baker in Bucharest, Romania. He immigrated with his family to Palestine in the late 1890s and was one of the founders of the village.

During the first years, he baked breads like the rest of the residents on wood-burning stoves. The wheat was bought from Arab farmers, who grew the poor grains. Eventually, the residents learned to grow good types of grain and used them for bread.

Weinschel decided that it was time he had made use of his Romanian knowledge. He and his son started looking for ovens. One day they received word that an old bakery in Tiberias had closed and its equipment was for sale. They found the bakery and its obsolete and crumbling equipment, and for a few Bishliks, purchased the oven, dismantled it, and led it on a caravan of mules to the village. None of the villages believed that bread would come out of the heap of scrap, but without faith, there would be no bread.

After much work, the knowledgeable father and diligent son were able to assemble and operate the baking oven on fuel oil. The first batch of bread was partially burnt and partly unbaked. In an ingenious marketing gesture, the Weinschels distributed the first batch of bread to the villagers free of charge.

The baking procedures gradually improved, and the villagers discovered that it was better for them to sell the wheat they had grown to Weinschels and buy baked bread from them. In the early days, the bakery only sold breads on Sundays and Thursdays. They made the big leap when the main bakery in Rosh Pina burned down. The residents there turned to the bakeries in Safed and to Weinschel and his son's bakery. Even after the restoration of the bakery in Rosh Pina, the bakery in the village continued to bake goods on a daily basis.

A bakery is a bakery, and a store is a store, and as already mentioned, there were no shops in Esther's village but in the metropolis of Rosh Pina. In the center of the commercial area stood the carriage station of Machenkin and his son. From here, carriages would depart, and transportation services were provided to Tiberias, Jerusalem, Safed, Haifa, Jaffa, Acre, and from there on to Beirut.

Machenkin's station included an office building on the top floor that offered six guest rooms. It was the first and only hotel in Rosh Pina. Separate stables were built around it for horses, camels, and mules, an animal hostel where they were given water and rest.

The stable area also included a military corral closed to the general public, which was formerly used by the Turkish army, but after they were defeated and fled, the British Army took control of the stable. The English paid the military horses great respect by allotting a special place for retired horses.

A designated groom treated the horses, brushed their tails, and polished their bodies. A beautiful black horse with a white star on its forehead, eyes blazing, and upright ears was given extra-special care.

"This is General Allenby's horse," said the groom proudly and in a whisper, violating the secrecy to which he was sworn.

Next to the stable was a large parking lot that was used for Machenkin's carriages, as well as a parking and rest area for passing coaches. The wagons stood in an orderly row including fancy decorated carriages for six, to simple wagons intended for a single passenger.

The compound included a paved area for various uses. Once a month, a dentist from Tiberias would arrive by mule, dressed in white, and a wide-brimmed hat on his head. He led another mule with his medical equipment, and when he reached the plaza, not far from the military stable, he would unload a dentists' chair and place a small cabinet and on it, pliers, and other frightening tools, waiting for patients.

That was the sign for the royal groom to lead Allenby's horse to the edge of the stable.

"The patients' cries of pain adversely affect the horse's teeth," he explained to those interested.

Near the transportation complex, a diligent entrepreneur opened a store by the name:

"The Forging"
Forging and renovation of camels, horses, and mules.
Each treatment – two MIL
People for free

Further down the street was a store topped with the sign: **"Houseware and Clothing"** In one part, rows of primuses, wicks, kettles with a selection of nozzles, pales, iron surfaces for the oven, plates of various types as well as plates from wood and ceramics, crates containing various cutlery utensils, tablecloths, and other kitchen items.

The other part of the store was for clothes and included various items for men and especially women. On one side stood a wooden rack holding hats, berets for school children, and secondhand cork hats, which probably once belonged to an elephant hunter. The other side of the store displayed women's clothing: long dresses, shirts, shoes in different sizes and colors, scarves, and used bras.

"Everything is secondhand," the seller explained after selling a bluish wick cooking stove.

Past the bakery further down, there was the candy and tobacco shop. In the late days of the war, sweets were scarce, however, there was plenty of tobacco and cigarettes to be found. A captive crowd of heavy smokers, the result of an ongoing war and mental stress, would frequent the shop.

With background knowledge of the rich commercial life of Rosh Pina, Esther began her work at NAAFI. The store was broad, gleaming, and flooded with light. Immediately after entering the store, on its east side, one would find the fruit and vegetable produce department. Esther was surprised to see it as there was no such thing in her village. Villagers would grow vegetables and fruit themselves and would exchange the surplus. The same was true in Rosh Pina, except for the Friday market, where the farmers would sell vegetables grown in their fields.

The tobacco and cigarettes were all on the western part of the shop. Here, too, she was in for a surprise. In Rosh Pina, one might find cigarettes made locally and the dusty shelves would be laden with branded packages of cigarettes such as "Camel," "Latif," "Amir," "Matossian," "Yasmin," and a few open boxes of "Nelson," as those cigarettes were pricier and would be sold individually. In complete contrast, the NAAFI tobacconist department was quite inviting. One section sold pipes made in England while in the next, tobacco packages of various sizes made in Cuba;

in the most attractive section of the department there was a display of leading cigarettes from all over the world. Esther did not know most of them, but it was enough for her to see the decks with the names "Kent," "Pal Mal," and "Lucky Strike," to understand that she had arrived in a different universe.

Joe or George noticed her enthusiasm and led her to the sweets department. Undoubtedly, Esther thought to herself, it would be worthwhile to serve in the British Army if only to enjoy the abundance of sweets and chocolate bars that filled the store. Coming from a world of scarcity at worst and austerity at best, she could not help but admire the piles of English "Cadbury" chocolate and the shelves full of Swiss chocolate, loaded with packs of "Toblerone" and "Sushard."

"The least we can do for our heroic soldiers is to give them the sense that there is someone indulging their families on the home front," George explained.

The food department was packed with tantalizing and enticing food items and included, among other things, Bully Beef in packs of three, French sausages, sardines from Portugal, and packaged salmon from Norway. Fresh breads and pastries were also to be found. These were provided to "NAAFI" by the nearby bakery, whose Christian-Armenian owner boasted a seven-generation family baking tradition.

Finally, in the beverage department, Esther was dazzled by the rich selection. The most popular drink was Scotch whiskey followed by French drinks, and a selection of beers from different countries.

The store was open Sunday through Friday from nine to five.

Most of the customers were women who used the free food stamps they received or others who came to indulge in specialty products.

"If you see a woman adding to her basket sausages, meats, and a bottle of 'Johnny Walker,' it's a sign that her husband is coming home on a two-week leave," George noted. "In that case, add a 'Cadbury' bar on the King's expense."

For the first few days, Esther would get to work in a clanky bus ride that lasted two hours. Soon however, Joe found a room in an Armenian family's house about a ten-minute walk from the shop, which made life shine more beautiful.

Her father was devastated about what was happening with his daughter. It was bad enough that his two sons had become priests, now his only daughter began to work in a store belonging to Gentiles. Hannah supported her husband outwardly but noticed a gleam that returned to Esther's eyes, a blush that rose again on her cheeks, and the joy that was in her heart.

Esther loved her job at the shop, and the shop loved her. A friendly bond was formed between Esther and her customers. They told her about their longing for their husbands and their excitement for them to be coming home soon. She quickly learned that when it comes to missing a loved one and excitement, there is no difference between Jewish, Christian, or Muslim women. The longings were felt the same and so were expectations.

Esther no longer needed the bottle of Johnny Walker to tell her about an impending leave, as the women shared their feelings with her and consulted with her about the pampering basket they would make for their husbands. The Cadbury packs, at the King's expense, made their way to the basket. Esther would drop into their basket two packs, knowing that out of the corner of his eye, George would notice her bend the rules.

The friendship between Esther and George deepened. He welcomed her contribution to the store's success, and the letters of thanks sent by shoppers to the chain's management only reinforced the feelings of appreciation and affection he felt for her.

One day Esther saw a small ad pasted on the billboard in the store: "The store's management invites the employees to a social gathering that will be held this coming Monday in the Carmel forests. Departure at nine in the morning from the shop."

Earlier that week, the two maintenance workers announced that they would not be joining due to a Muslim holiday that fell on that same day, and the English cashier announced toward the end of Thursday that she felt an impending migraine attack and would not attend either.

On Sunday morning, Esther arrived at the shop at fifteen minutes before nine. George was already there, standing next to a blue Vauxhall with white wheels and a right-hand steering wheel. He wore his forever trousers, a plaid shirt, and a Scottish tartan flat cap topped with a pompom.

"Is it okay for us to travel alone?" he asked her in a cheerful voice.

Esther, wearing an orange skirt, yellow tank top, and black bolero, clothes she bought especially for the occasion at the "Housewares and Clothing" store in Rosh Pina, did not bother to answer the question. She feared that the melody of the words would compromise her joy and excitement.

George entered the store and came out with a large straw basket filled with groceries, two bottles of beer, and one bottle of wine, and placed them on the back leather seat of the Vauxhall. He turned to the left front door of the car, opened it wide, and in a chivalrous gesture invited Esther in, making sure to close the door behind her.

Esther was overwhelmed. No one had ever treated her with the utmost respect and politeness as George did. She had long since failed to define her feelings for him, and now she seemed to have the answer in hand, and it shook her to her core.

The car climbed to the top of Mount Carmel. Small cottages dotted the sides of the road. The ones on the left overlooked the beautiful Haifa Bay stretching from Haifa to Acre, a crescent of sea, and the houses on the right enjoyed the view of the coast from Haifa to the Crusader Fortress of Atlit in the south. Esther, who had never been to the Carmel before, moved her head from side to side, thrilled by the stunning scenery.

At one point, George slowed down and continued down a dirt path that blended into the heart of the landscape. The path narrowed and made its way between pine and elm trees until it was blocked by a huge rock.

Is this the destination of the social gathering planned for the store employees? Esther asked herself, but immediately regained her composure remembering that, not everything needs to be asked and not everything needs to be known.

George seemed to know his way, driving the car down a half-hidden path that evaded the rock, and continued driving another fifty feet, to a small patch of heaven. It was covered with low green grass and surrounded by tall pine trees that shared the area with lentisk bushes. Cyclamen flowers of late autumn and vibrant early-season anemones came together in a stunning tapestry of colors.

George stopped the car near the patch, being careful not to disturb its quaintness. He took a colorful blanket out of the trunk and spread it out on the grass. On the blanket, he placed the wicker basket he had taken out of the car. Bees buzzed in the air, flying over the abundance of flowers surrounding them.

"Every bee has its quota," George said, following her gaze. "A bee that has had its fill of cyclamen nectar will not mix it with anemone sap."

He invited Esther to lie down next to him on the blanket, and took off his high shoes and socks, which he'd kept since his time in the military. His muscular white calves and concave feet evoked a burst of emotion in her.

She, who had only ever lived with a father and two older brothers, was amazed at the intensity of the excitement that rushed through her body at the sight of his exposed body parts.

George pretended not to notice the outburst of emotion that flooded Esther. He slowly took the bottle of wine out of the basket, removed the cork, and poured one glass of wine for the both of them. He brought the glass between their heads in an attempt to sip the same glass together, but the glass did not reach its destination. Not knowing how it had happened, their lips met in a passionate, loving kiss.

All Esther remembered in that moment of lust was to untie the lanyard that held George's trousers, and to leave him to take them off. However, the job was not completed. Underneath, George wore boxer shorts over an impressive bulge. The task was divided between the two. Esther pounced on the boxers with the intention of setting the bulge free, while George focused on her bra.

Even in that moment, Esther did not forget to be thankful for her good fortune. In the days before this outing, she went down to Rosh Pina to the "Housewares and Clothing" store and asked to buy a bra that would tighten her breasts. All the saleswomen had to offer was a size four secondhand bra.

"It's too big for me," Estherka complained.

"What's the problem?" the saleswoman replied. "Do as everyone else. Take some wool and fill in the gap between the breasts and the bra, and then you will get big and firm breasts for the same price."

Now, Esther was horrified at how many tufts of wool George would have had to gather from her breasts to reach her nipples, if she had taken the saleswoman's advice. Breasts were exposed, nipples were licked, the bulge released and led by the hand of a master to Esther's entrance, who received him with a tremor of lust and passion. She was not a virgin prior to her sweeping encounter with George.

In one of the matchmaking dates, she met with a student from a reputed yeshiva in Safed. As part of the acquaintance process, they walked through the ancient cemetery of Safed, and in the evening, in the face of the spectacular sunset over the Galilee mountains, they found themselves leaning over, him with his pants rolled down to his knees, and her in a dress raised up to the waist, having sex.

That relationship ended as soon as the student heard that he would have to invite two priests to Seder night in all the years ahead once they were married and that simply did not resonate with him. But she remembered the student for the better. He released her from inhibitions and hesitations, allowing herself to be carried away passionately by George.

The sun was about to set. A lone pinecone cracked and scattered its seeds everywhere. The industrious bees crowded around their queen. And with her sharpened senses, Esther heard the cyclamen greeting their anemone neighbors with a good night's blessing.

Esther and George remembered that they had yet to eat. They pounced on the groceries inside the straw basket and devoured its contents.

During work, Esther avoided eating from the store's delicacies for kosher reasons, but today she removed all restrictions and consumed life, from promising puffs to sausage delicacies from Germany, wrapped in French cheese from Montpellier.

The sun deepened its sunset. The two quickly collected their belongings, got into the blue car with the white wheels and hurried back to Haifa.

***

The following weeks were as sweet as honey. Esther hovered happily gulping up the looks of love sent to her from the manager's humble room. Every day she looked forward to her night encounters with her lover.

The owners of the apartment where she lived forbade her to host anyone in her room, so the lovers would meet in the small and pleasant service apartment that the company put up for George's use, near the port of Haifa and a short walk from the shop. She would see her parents only once every two weeks, saying it was due the shop being so busy.

In their encounters, Esther and George shared their time in stormy acts of love and indulging their fondness for the culinary treats the store had to offer. From time to time they would visit a sailor bar near the apartment, quenching their thirst with a cold bottle of beer.

Until that one bitter and rushed day.

Esther was waiting for him in the apartment, enjoying a delightful view.

George paused and when he arrived, his shoulders hunched over, his eyes lowered, and a strange smell of beer wafted from his mouth.

"What happened?" she asked.

He did not reply. Vague feelings of fear climbed up her body. She had never seen him as low and shrunken as at that moment.

"What happened?" she asked again.

The nebulous feelings were replaced by sharp stabs. He remained silent. Anxiety paralyzed her. She felt her life was about to change.

After prolonged silence he said, "I will be returning to London tomorrow."

The atmosphere in the apartment plummeted to gloom and so did her heart.

"But just today you sent me messages of love... what has changed?"

"The chain decided to close the store in Haifa and lay off all employees at the end of the war," he said.

Tall George with the laughing eyes and beloved face was gone, and a stranger stood before her.

"When did you find out? Why didn't you tell me?" She was looking for a glimmer of hope.

"I was scared," he told her. "And besides, I want to visit my wife and children."

Darkness descended on her soul. George the chatterbox told her everything, she thought, from stories about Eva's kindergarten teacher to the names of his gay friends at Cambridge. Yet he had never mentioned a wife and children.

Nausea gripped her. She felt an urgent need to vomit.

George got up, stingily stroked her hair, kissed her cheek, and said, "Don't worry, we'll keep in touch."

Esther stood up and crawled out of the apartment. She hurled her guts out in the hallway. She did not remember how and what, but after three days she woke up in her own bed in the village to her worried mother placing a cold towel on her forehead and whispering to her words of encouragement and love.

CHAPTER 8 – KING DAVID

The "Jewish priest," as David was called behind his back, was highly revered.

St. Michael's Church was considered a leading church. The congregation would gather not only from Newcastle but also from farther areas. One day, principals from the theological seminary came to the church to meet with a graduate of the seminary and learn how he had made the church a magnet for believers and a role model for other churches.

"I'll have you know," said one of the bishops. "That every year there is a competition among our graduates for the right to serve in your church."

His brother, Shmuel, now Samuel, as he was known under his new identity, also made a name for himself in the Christian establishment. As a researcher at the Theological Seminary in London, he focused on a comparative study between Christianity and Judaism. His research had received mixed, critical responses from the Catholic Church, and sympathy from the Anglican and Protestant Churches.

The brothers made sure to meet twice a year. On Yom Kippur, they used to meet at David's apartment in

Newcastle. They prayed the Jewish prayer of "Kol Nidrei" and kept the fast. Passover would be celebrated in Samuel's London apartment, which would be kosher as customary. They conducted Seder night by the rules and divided among themselves the four questions of "Ma Nishtana," asking: "What makes tonight different from all other nights?"

The longing for parents and their little sister was the central theme in these meetings. They both hoped and prayed to meet with them again one day. They never expressed remorse for their conversion to Christianity and never denied their Jewish origins.

"I know I was born a Jew, that I live as a Christian, and that I will die as a Jew," David told his brother more than once. "What about you?"

"I feel like a Jew loaned to Christianity," his brother replied.

****

The darkness that fell on the world during World War II did not pass over Newcastle. At first, the civil defense services ordered all public institutions to dim the lights in the buildings, but as the war continued, such bans increased. In the final year of the war, David served in a church with windows blackened with parchment paper and doors supported by wooden beams. The heavy blitz suffered by London did not reach the city on a large scale, however, the occasional bombings, the austerity regime, and the general heavy feeling of war were enough to keep worshipers in their homes.

At the end of the war, thousands of people took to the streets in celebration, and the masses of worshipers returned to the church to give thanks. Since the war had broken out, the church had not enjoyed such a renaissance. Three months later, a uniformed major in the British Air Force entered the church and approached David.

"I want to talk to you," he said.

In those days, uniformed personnel symbolized victory. They were carried on shoulders and received such respect as is usually reserved for priests in St. Michael's Church.

"Come, step into my office." David invited him with great pride and respect.

"I am here on a mission," said the officer. "The people of London want to meet you."

"To what do I owe this honor?" David was amazed.

"I'm not allowed to tell you, but if they sent me here as they did, you could assume it's a matter of importance."

"How urgent is it?"

"Urgent enough to let you know that the meeting is scheduled to take place in three days at the War Office on Bond Street in central London."

The distance between Newcastle and London was only two hundred eighty-five miles yet it took the train five hours to get there. From the train station, David boarded a double-decker bus that drove him to the entrance to the *Ministry of Defense building*. There was no sign of anything that would hint to what the occupants would be doing inside it. Only the number of the building, and that was it.

David identified himself and provided his details. An army officer led him to a modest lobby and invited him to wash off the journey and help himself to some sandwiches that were set out on a round table. After eating a lettuce and tomato sandwich and drinking the obligatory tea, he was invited to an adjoining room.

A highly decorated general sat at the head of an elongated table, and to its side, four other officers of varying ranks.

"Mr. David Meisels," the general addressed him. "You must want to know why we brought you all the way from Newcastle, and why I address you by your given name and not by your ecclesiastical title, and of course, what we could possibly want from you, am I right?"

"All true," David replied, looking directly at the general and the officers around him, starting to realize that for him the war was just beginning.

"Straight to the point," said the general. "We are a subcommittee on Middle East intelligence, and we operate within the British War Office."

"Sounds interesting," David replied. "But what do you want from me?"

"So, the thing is, the war has ended in victory for Britain and the United States, but we are paying a heavy price and facing various problems around the world. British intelligence was prepared an overview on Great Britain's status in the world and the challenges ahead... one of the most delicate areas that they have pointed out is the Middle East with all of its problems and risks. In order to deal with these matters, the intelligence department set up working groups, and all of us sitting in this room, were tasked with dealing with the Middle East."

"Okay..." David replied. "And what has that to do with me?"

"In a brief examination of the subject before us, we have discovered that Britain has no intelligence infrastructure in the Middle East."

David began to lose patience, his clerical collar felt tight around his neck. "But what would a humble priest from Newcastle have to do with the intelligence war you're talking about?" he asked.

"I'm getting to that," the general continued to speak calmly. "Intelligence is based on intelligence. We checked and found that in Newcastle there is one called David Meisels and he speaks the languages Hebrew, Arabic, English, and Yiddish, and that is exactly what we are looking for. Since intelligence is important even on the smallest of details, we deepened our research and found that this Newcastle fellow possesses the traits best fitted for the job."

David took a deep breath, without succumbing to the glares straight at him and asked, "So what are we talking about?"

"We would like to appoint you Chief Intelligence Adviser at our branch in the Middle East."

"But I am a vicar with a church and a parish!"

"Everything has been taken into account," one of the officers interjected. "We have received the archbishop's consent to release you from church duties for the sake of three years of national service."

David was slightly stunned.

"You have two weeks," the general declared. "To settle all your personal affairs and hand over the reins to the vicar that has already been chosen to replace you. After that, you shall return to London where we will sit together and prepare a work plan and missions for you once you're in Palestine."

Two weeks and another passed, and David boarded a ship headed for Palestine, not before he went to see his brother in London.

"I have something to tell you." he said immediately after their embrace. "I'm being sent on government business to Palestine for a few years."

"What business?" Samuel asked.

"Intelligence Adviser."

"What would a vicar have to do with military intelligence?"

"I was shocked too," he replied. "They found me based on my language skills and my acquaintance with the people. I could not refuse the request, and it can certainly be an interesting revelation for me. Most of all, it is an opportunity for both of us. Perhaps the war has softened Dad a bit."

Samuel hugged his brother and sent him off wishing him success. They agreed that the next time they met would be in Palestine.

***

The voyage was pleasant. A car with a driver was waiting at the exit of the port of Haifa to take him to the King David hotel in Jerusalem.

The King David Hotel was indeed the most luxurious hotel in Palestine that boasted important guests, luxurious restaurants, and high room occupancy all year round, however, the war had taken its toll. Guests dwindled and revenue plummeted. In those days, the British Mandate authorities that controlled Palestine decided to make the hotel their headquarters.

As part of the emergency laws they had instated, British authorities issued a seizure order under which the entire southern part of the hotel was expropriated in their favor and the owners could not do much to object. The hotel was empty as it were, and they secretly hoped that the British presence would breathe life into it. The hotel soon became the center of English activity in Palestine. Hundreds of English civilians and soldiers manned the southern wing, and from there all the orders of British military and civilian administration were carried out and orchestrated, while the hotel ran regularly in its other parts.

Upon arriving in Palestine, David established his residence and center of his operation at King David.

In June 1946, Samuel informed him that he had gladly accepted his invitation to stay at his hotel, and that he intended to visit within the next month.

***

"I heard you were ill," Kurtzman said to Ester as she sat across from him in his office at the station. "But the doctor I brought to you said you would be fine."

"I'm okay and I'll be even better once you put me in touch with the guys fighting the British," she replied.

Kurtzman looked at her with knowing eyes and said with a slight nod, "They will call you."

Days passed and one of Kurtzman's carriage drivers appeared with a sealed envelope containing a note: Tuesday, at noon.

"Kurtzman told me to tell you in person," the messenger stated. "82 Herzl Street, Tel Aviv."

Esther was looking forward to the meeting. Vengeance burned inside her, and she knew that it would be the only way to save her from the abyss into which she had fallen. George's image merged with the British as a whole. Despair, frustration, hatred, and insult burned her soul, and an unfamiliar need for retribution filled her whole being.

On Herzl Street she was greeted warmly. "We heard good things about you, we need women like you," they told her.

She started her career in the organization in small operations. Posting leaflets against the British government, distributing flyers in mailboxes, and recruiting new members to the organization. After a short period of basic training, she began advanced firing training that included live fire in a shooting range out on the dunes of Caesarea.

Her first engagement in actual combat was a night ambush for a British supply convoy traveling on the Acre-Haifa Road, in which the fighters caused heavy damage to the caravan. As the days passed, the confidence of her commanders in her grew stronger, and Esther was trusted with many missions.

One day she attended a special staff meeting at the organization's headquarters in Tel Aviv. The meeting was convened after the failure of one of the operations, which left many casualties.

"We need to come up with a quick and substantial act of retribution," the organization's operations officer said. "Serious action must be taken to shock the English. We have prepared a plan that includes a real blow to one of the prominent symbols of the British occupation, and we are working today to complete the plan."

After that meeting, Esther approached the operations officer. "What's missing?" she asked.

The commander looked at her in amazement and appreciation, and after a slight hesitation told her, "We are looking for the best way to insert explosives into the King David Hotel in Jerusalem."

"Let me give it some thought," she said.

"Have a good day," he replied, as he turned away.

Esther stayed in Tel Aviv. She spent the night on a mattress rolled out on the floor of her comrade's rented apartment. Deep in her thoughts, she would not sleep the entire night.

The following morning, she sent a message to the man she met about her wish to confer with him soon. The meeting would take place on a particular bench along the Tel Aviv promenade. Once they were both certain they were not being surveilled and that they could be heard only by the passing seagulls, they sat down.

The operations officer, a short man with a sharp face plowed with wrinkles, stared at her, questioning.

Esther sent a worried look at the seagulls, for it would not be too farfetched that they would be in service of the enemy, then bent down and whispered in the commander's ear, "Milk jugs."

The commander, who was told that the ice resides in his arteries and that no encounter with death or with love would ever make his brow move, perked his ears, and opened his eyes wide.

Esther threw a stone at the seagulls and drove them away, then came closer to the commander's ear and whispered to him whatever she did. Minutes later, she would get up and rush to catch the bus to Rosh Pina, leaving the commander stunned in his seat on the lone bench on the Tel Aviv promenade.

Several days later, a "Ford" van appeared in the village. Esther waited for it at the entrance gate and guided the driver to the front door of the abandoned dairy. The driver, a sturdy young man, took six jugs out of the dairy, loaded them into the van, covered them with jute bags, and drove out of the village.

＊＊＊

After an exhausting flight, Shmuel's plane landed late at night at Wilhelma Airport, near the city of Lod. He boarded a taxi to the King David Hotel in Jerusalem and arrived there early in the morning.

The sleepy receptionist gave him the key to the pre-booked room, along with a note: "Excited for our meeting. See you at 11:30 on the hotel balcony. Dudi."

Prior to the meeting, Shmuel put on his elegant priest's outfit, walked down and out to the balcony that dominated the entire eastern area of the lobby. A tall Sudanese waiter led him to his brother's seat in a corner on the south side of the terrace.

The meeting between the brothers was filled with excitement. After a long embrace, the two sat down, flooded with stories they were about to share with one another.

"We don't have much time," Dudi said. "We have a meeting with the High Commissioner. He is eager to meet you after all the stories I've told him about you."

Samuel left it to Dudi to order him a meal and even before it ended, he told him, "You owe me something."

Dudi laughed. "There are things I do not forget..."

He pointed his finger at the tall waiter and said, "We're in a hurry, but I promised Shmuel we would not leave without taking a bite out of our trifle," Dudi said.

"I didn't need much convincing... the truth is that I came here solely because word of the trifle you serve here has made its way all the way to London."

"It's going to take a quarter of an hour. We don't have a trifle ready as we only make it to order," the waiter said.

"The goal justifies the time," Shmuel replied with a sigh, glancing at his watch.

The waiter nodded his head and rushed to the kitchen.

At twelve twenty-five, Shmuel went to the restroom and when he came out, he saw the waiter carrying in one hand two stunningly colorful dishes. When he got to the middle of the balcony, he heard a massive explosion and right in front of his terrified eyes he saw the southern part of the terrace collapse and his brother disappear into the abyss.

"My brother! My brother," he screamed in horror, not noticing the fire that had gripped his elegant priestly clothes.

Shmuel was evacuated along with other people to the lobby, where he provided his details and those of his missing brother and then underwent a medical examination.

Deemed unharmed, he was escorted to his hotel room.

He threw out the remains of his burnt clothes, showered, and lay on the bed riddled with pain and yearning.

A few hours later he was asked to go down to the intelligence center set up on the entrance floor, which was divided into several areas. The dining room was converted into a huge morgue, and the bodies or remains of the bodies of ninety-one of the victims of the explosion were lined up in straight rows, covered with white sheets. The entrance to the terrace was blocked off with ropes.

Investigators wandered around among the remains looking for evidence as to what might have led to the explosion.

One corner of the lobby had been turned into a triage. Dozens of doctors and nurses provided first aid to hundreds injured and sent them in howling ambulances to the various hospitals in the city.

The lobby itself was blocked and only officials – police and government, as well as journalists from all over the world – were allowed to enter.

Shmuel approached the information center established in the middle of the lobby, and after identifying himself, a staff member accompanied him to the morgue. He found his brother at the beginning of the second row, lying with his eyes closed, covered with a sheet up to his chin, his head intact and hock plastered on his face.

"Yes, I know the man," he replied in a broken voice. "It's my brother."

He was then escorted to the information desk, where he was offered a chair and a glass of water. After filling out a number of forms, he was approached by one of the army officers standing at the scene:

"We are sorry for your family's loss, but in this painful moment, we must receive the family's instructions regarding burial arrangements..."

A flash of consciousness set his thoughts straight. He recalled the words of his brother, there, at a church in Newcastle: "I was born a Jew and I will die as a Jew."

"I want to bury my brother in the cemetery at the village of Yesodot," Shmuel replied to the officer standing in front of him, honored to be able to fulfill his brother's wishes.

***

Shmuel's soul bowed. The sight of his brother's face, the long white lines, the bloodstains, the human commotion in the lobby, and an indistinct emotion that immerged in his heart ordered him to leave. He did not want to go up to his room. It was cozy yet compact and lacked any intimacy. A low table, two faux armchairs, a long window facing the back of the hotel, and three uninspired landscape photos hung on the walls.

He went outside. On the other side of the hotel stood the YMCA Tower, which was included among the ten most beautiful YMCA buildings in the world, and on its southern side was a beautiful well-kept garden.

Shmuel sat down on a bench between two tall cypress trees and allowed himself to sink into its wreckage. The sadness and pain moved with the hum of the trees and were replaced with the satisfaction that his brother would be buried as he wished, according to Jewish law.

With a sense that he had paid the debt he had to himself, Shmuel got up from the bench, crossed the garden, and returned to the hotel. He went up to his room and prepared for a long journey. Before leaving the room, he packed his spare clergy garments, went down to the reception, and explained to the concierge what to do with the package he had left behind in the room.

***

Monsignor Galeto Plova Tyrminis, the bishop's secretary, looked curiously at the package delivered to his office by a special courier from the Jerusalem Central Post Office on Jaffa Street. He placed the large cardboard box on the small sitting table in the corner of the office, grabbed a silver envelope knife and opened it. To his amazement, he found in it two sets of priests' garments and other religious items. The top set was an A class outfit. It included a long crimson robe, a gilded sash, and a large robe, matching cap, and collar topped with a white strip.

Underneath this set was a folded set of a vicar's work clothes. A white long-sleeved shirt starched and neatly ironed, a short jacket, long trousers, and a matching cap, all in black. This pile was also topped with a black collar and a white strip.

Next to the clothes was a large bronze cross attached to a long necklace, all handmade, and right by that, another pectoral cross for everyday use. A note was on the bottom of the package:

To the Honorable Bishop of Jerusalem,

I hereby thank you for the long and fascinating years of shared faith, in which I learned about the meaning of patience, friendship, and the acceptance of the other.

I want to tell you that after a mental quandary with myself, and following a terrible personal tragedy I have suffered, I concluded that my place is with the Jewish faith, where I came from.

I thank you, all my fellow priests and all my friends, for containing me over the years, for the understanding and warmth I have received.

Given my decision, I shall not have use for the included items, and I am sure you will put them to better use.

With thanks and appreciation,

Shmuel Meisels

Formally known as Samuel Meisels

The day after the explosion, after a sleepless night, Shmuel arrived at the station in Jerusalem, where he boarded the bus to Tiberias and at the station waited for the coach that would later leave for Safed.

CHAPTER 9 – YESODOT

Heat fumes rose from the Sea of Galilee and wrapped the bus stop in a thick layer of humidity. Shmuel sat on a wooden bench by the platform. The bus to Safed was already at the station attracting much of a commotion.

An Arab porter climbed a ladder on the back of the bus and lifted the passengers' luggage onto the roof, where his assistant would tie the luggage to the iron frame to keep it from falling during the shaky ride. The porter struggled on the narrow ladder, the dreadful heat, and the heavy-set woman watching over his work whose yells could be heard from one side of the station to the other.

"Watch out for my China!" she shouted in a hoarse voice. "You're ruining my life!"

The bus painted in red and white had a long nose that contained a six-cylinder gasoline engine made by Ford. A short man, who would turn out to be the driver, poured buckets of water on the hood to cool it down ahead of the ride.

"What does he think he's doing?" Shmuel mumbled as he watched the water turn to steam as soon as it touched the hot metal.

After the porters had finished their work, the two porters approached the driver and received from him a few coins for their trouble. The driver sat down on his seat, and through the open door shouted at the tired passengers waiting at the bus entrance. "The 'Tepaleh' for Safed is about to leave!"

The Yiddish word for a cooking pot suited the situation perfectly. The bus body was made mostly of wood built at the "Argaz" factory and mounted on a chassis manufactured by Ford, while the bus ceiling was made of heat-absorbing tin that gave passengers a feeling that they were crowded inside a pot of broth placed on the stove on a Friday.

Each passenger would pay the driver coins he would divide by size into long silver cylinders, and in return received a card that the driver punctured with a special hole puncher he would hold in his hand. The bus boasted ten wooden benches designed for twenty passengers. Behind the driver's seat, above the bench, was a sign reminding passengers to allow the elderly priority seating.

Shmuel noticed that the place was occupied by a young couple adjoined by the sandals and nothing elderly about them. Before the ride had begun, they had already put their heads on top of each other and slept the entire journey.

Shmuel, who was among the first to board the bus, looked at the passengers getting onto the bus in horror. The heavy-set woman sat down next to him and occupied a hefty chunk of his seat. At one point he thought of changing seats, though he soon realized they were all taken. She had only just sat down and already begun to complain about the promiscuous porters who did not treat her belongings with the respect their deserved. Her lofty words were accompanied by splashes of saliva.

Shmuel looked hopefully at the sign placed above the seats along the bus: "Do not spit on the floor."

The bus was ready to go. At the very last minute, two rabbinical students in long black clothes hopped in. Since all the seats were occupied, they had to hold on tightly to leather straps that hung from the ceiling meant for standing commuters.

At one point Shmuel thought to suggest a swap, but soon gave up on the idea. They are younger and had also paid half price for a ticket standing up, he told himself.

The bus driver got up, surveyed the passengers, and checked that everything was in order before he sat down in his seat and pulled a handle that activated the closing mechanism of the bus door. The engine coughed lightly and stabilized. The bus set off, from Bethsaida Valley and began to climb the mountain. The driver kept his hand on the lever that was steady in first gear, promising the groaning bus that once they would have made it up hill, he would indulge it straight into second gear. The narrow road, sharp bends, and bumps put the passengers to sleep.

"Rosh Pina Station!" the driver exclaimed out loud.

Shmuel awoke in a daze, only to find that he had fallen asleep on the left breast of his bench partner, who was still very much asleep. All the passengers got off, most of which would carry on to Safed, while Shmuel and three other new passengers boarded a bus to Metula.

Shmuel sat alone on a bench and gazed at the familiar view. Approaching Yesodot, he pulled on the wire that ran along the bus and rang a bell by the driver's seat. The vehicle stopped at the entrance to the village and Shmuel was the only passenger to step out.

I have to find a place to rest and collect myself before meeting my parents, he thought, and yes, yes... to allow my father to finish his mandatory afternoon nap.

The entrance to the village remained exactly the same. A strip of dense gravel from the main road to near the synagogue. The first house on the right, white with blue shutters and a rose garden, was the home of the Blumenthal family. Shmuel recalled his childhood days, when the villagers thought they would make a living by producing perfumes from flowers under their chosen trade name "Myr Balm."

The Blumenthal family was one of the leaders in the industry. They continued to grow roses even after the commercial failure, when no perfume buyers were found, not in Paris or even in Rosh Pina. Across the road stood the Machenkin family home. The houses were far apart, each surrounded by a broad estate. Shmuel was not at all surprised to see a red car with a long nose and a roof made of coarse cloth at the entrance to the Machenkin's estate. The Machenkin family managed and led the transportation sector in the village.

In the village's first years, the link with the outside world was maintained on the backs of camels and donkeys. Some of the camels would drag carriers on the ground behind them. The father of the Machenkin family was the first transportation entrepreneur in the village. He built himself a cart in a carpentry shop in Rosh Pina, assembled four wheels made of wood, and harnessed it to a mule he had bought in an Arab village near Rosh Pina. The success of the venture was immense. In exchange for pennies paid by villagers, who were happy to be carted around rather than suffer the butt cramps and back aches from riding camels and donkeys.

However, then the transportation crisis hit, and it was tragic. One day, Machenkin was called to transfer a fever-stricken patient to the doctor in Rosh Pina. In the middle of the road, the mule decided that he'd had enough of the hard work and stopped walking. All attempts to make him carry on, whether mean or kind – failed. The stubborn mule would not move. In the end there was no choice but to move the miserable patient to Rosh Pina on the back of a donkey, and when they got to the doctor, he had no choice but to call the patient's time of death.

The rage in the village was great, and for a short time camels and donkeys were again seen on the main street of Yesodot. Yet the dramatic solution was soon to come. Months later, one spring morning, a magnificent two-horse stagecoach appeared on the main street of the village, and in front of it was a large sign: "Machenkin and son – Diligence Services"

It was a real transportation revolution. The Diligence stagecoach was made of a wooden body on four wheels mounted with shock-absorbing springs. A wide wooden bench was placed along the side of the cart, and three people could sit on it on each side, back-to-back. At the end of the carriage there was room for luggage and each passenger would be allowed to board with a cargo weighing up to two rotels. For extra weight the passenger would pay twenty-two pennies more per rotel, with the total weight per person restricted to five rotels.

The Machenkin family's stagecoaches traveled on the Rosh Pina line, where they would join a network of stagecoaches that expanded in those days to the country. The village council adapted to the changing conditions, broadened the entrance to the village and poured gravel on it, but the arrival of the stagecoach tore the residents into two camps divided on the question: who was responsible for cleaning and collecting horse manure that filled the street.

After deliberations, including threats to take the dispute to a religious court of law, the village council committee and the Machenkin family reached a compromise that the expenditure would be divided between the parties in equal parts. As early as the next day, the fare prices rose to the cover the Machenkin's end of the deal.

Shmuel continued to walk down the empty street. The houses on both sides sent him down memory lane. Further down the road, near the synagogue and in front of his parents' house, he saw a large tree casting its shadow all over the street. An emotion choked his throat. It was the mulberry tree.

Ever since he identified his brother's body at the King David Hotel in Jerusalem, he could not shake the image out of his mind and now, it was hitting him even harder. Only the bench under the tree stopped him from falling unconscious on the hot ground.

When he and his brother were children, in search of a way to make a living, the villagers entertained an idea put forward by the emissaries of Lord Rothschild, a well-known gentleman who undertook to assist the developing villages throughout the Land of Israel. The Lord's representatives set up a silk factory in Rosh Pina, based on growing silkworms brought from China. The mulberries needed for industry were collected by workers in nearby and distant Arab villages.

The factory managers made an offer before the village council that they could not be refuse. "Let's grow mulberry trees," they were told. "And we promise to buy the leaves from you at a price that will cover your expenses and leave you a handsome profit."

The council gladly accepted the offer. Hundreds of mulberry seedlings were bought at the Mikve Israel agricultural school and sent to the village in special carts. On Tu BiShvat,[8] all the residents gathered in front of the rabbi's house for a ceremony celebrating the first tree planting. The rabbi's eldest son was chosen to plant the first tree, and in honor

---

8. **Tu BiShvat** also known as the Jewish 'New Year of the Trees' celebrating trees and plants.

of the occasion, his mother bought him a new white shirt. Shmuel took out the plant from its can and showed it to the crowd, but suddenly Dudi jumped up and snatched the seedling from him, informing the stunned audience that he would be the one planting the first seeding. Tumultuous minutes went by until the rabbi finally reached a compromise where both boys would plant the tree together.

After that, the entire village was filled with mulberry trees. The residents of Yesodot followed every bud and every leaf and calculated the huge profits that were about to fall into their laps. Disappointingly, after two years of operation, the factory in Rosh Pina went bankrupt and closed its gates, before a single leaf would be picked.

Eventually, the residents learned how to grow unique fruits suited for the weather conditions and the local soil. The fate of the mulberry trees was decided, and they were uprooted in favor of the new crops – plums, pears, and also apples, whose reputation spread all over the country.

One mulberry tree was left for posterity in commemoration of village history – Shmuel and Dudi's tree.

Shmuel sat under the tree. The tears he thought had all been dried up soaked his eyes once again. The sun shifted west, and a good breeze swept from the Golan Heights. He got up from the bench and crossed the street straight to his parents' house. He noticed that the driveway was different. It was no longer a tight clay path, but pebbles brought from the Sea of Galilee. Even the young Washingtonian trees he remembered from their youth had trunks reaching far and up to the azure sky.

The front door, made of oak and painted brown remained the same. Time took its toll leaving tiny grooves and perforations all over. It's time it was replaced, the thought went through his head.

Above the door was a sign:

"Shlomo Meisels – Rabbi of the Village"

His wrists froze, his fingers trembled, refusing to obey. He stood for many moments in front of the closed door until he managed to overcome his shudder. He took off his wide-brimmed hat, pulled a black yarmulke out of his pocket, placed it on his head, and knocked on the door.

The seconds passed like an eternity. The door opened. His mother stood in the doorway, silent and astonished. She took three steps back, looked over his shoulder and whispered, "Did you bring Dudi?"

Her hair had turned white, wrinkles of anger lined her forehead, two wrinkles ran down her mouth, but her eyes were the same eyes that illuminated everything in their surroundings, just as they did thirty years ago, when she commanded him as they parted, "Go get Dudi!"

His father, hunched over a holy book as usual, looked almost lifeless, tried to get up, though the burden of the years and the many ailments kept him in his chair.

"Shmuel!" A cry came out of his mouth. Bowed and white, his forehead lined with wrinkles and his tired eyes highlighting the time that had passed.

Shmuel tried to reach out long arms that would contain his two beloved parents.

"I have returned home," he said with the remainder of his strength.

"And what about Dudi?"

"Dudi is gone."

"I know..." Hannah said. "He died yesterday. My heart told me."

She collapsed on the couch behind her.

Shmuel hugged his mother and whispered in great tears, "He was on his way to you."

"I want him here, close to me..." She looked up at her husband.

The rabbi rose slowly to his feet, and with a hunched back, hobbled to leave the house assisted by a table. At the entrance to the house, he took the walking cane, put on a black hat, and said, "I'm off to evening prayers."

"I want to come with you," Shmuel said, checking the yarmulke's grip of his head.

"No," his father replied. "I want you to stay with Mom."

Hugging and sobbing, Shmuel and his mother sat on the couch. He told her about Dudi's last moments, his great love for his parents, and his plan to surprise them.

Silence took over the house. Shmuel closed his eyes while his entire life flashed before him. The scents of his childhood and of his mother, the comfort of home, and the sight of his father in his old age, all came together in heartbreak.

The shadows outside spread longer and with them the silence throughout the house. The door opened and the old father shuffled to his regular seat, over the scriptures.

After resting a little, he looked up at his wife and son and said in a low voice, "A son of Israel, despite sin is still a son of Israel. Our beloved son will be buried beside us." He burst into a great and liberating sob.

**

Conifers and oak had cast their shadow over the cemetery, leaving small slices of light for winter anemones and spring cyclamen. In the front row of the cemetery stood tombstones covered in greenish moss, bearing faded letters that tell the story of the founders of the village.

An atmosphere of relaxation and completeness prevailed in the cemetery, except for one area. A piece of land surrounded by a fence with the sign "Children's plot" located in the northern part of the cemetery, which attracted many visitors who were swept away by the story that enhanced emotions and scorched souls.

The founders of Yesodot fought the battles for their existence with great optimism. Between the mulberry leaves and rose blossoms they would always hope for the best. All would pale in the face of the merciless fever. The first afflicted by the disease were young children, whose immune system could not withstand the cruel mosquito fever. Many children died from the disease. Some buried without a name, placed in the ground in unmarked graves. Eventually, the plot was surrounded by a fence and made into a solemn site of remembrance.

Dudi's grave was dug next to it.

Circled in their grief, Shlomo and Hannah, Shmuel, and Esther stood by the grave. At a safe distance, stood the bishop of the Anglican Church from Jerusalem in a priest's uniform, and beside him an English Field Marshal wearing the gleaming uniform of the Royal Air Force.

The bishop stepped forward and bowed his head in a whisper, "Let your soul ascend to heaven and find its rest there." And added in Hebrew the Jewish blessing over the dead, "Baruch Dayan HaEmet."

The British General saluted and said, "On behalf of His Majesty and the Government of Great Britain, I salute Officer David Meisels for his contribution to His Majesty, the British Empire, and the entire free world."

The rabbi stood over the grave, stooped and stilled. His wife and son hurried to support him from both his sides.

"Yitgadal v'yitkadash sh'mei raba..." the father began saying Kaddish.[9] His voice faded with the words until he was no longer heard.

Shmuel finished the prayer in his stead, "He who makes peace in his high places will make peace on us and on all Israel and they shall say Amen."

The entire congregation, many of the residents of Yesodot, Bedouins, Arabs from neighboring villages, rabbis, students from Safed and Tiberias, priests, and clerics from all over the Galilee and even Jerusalem, answered together in tears and grief, "Amen"

**

---

9. **Kaddish** is the Jewish mourner's prayer, recited in the Aramaic language.

Many visitors came to comfort the mourners. Shmuel did not know most of them and assumed that they must be among the acquaintances of his parents and sister.

His father sat the majority of the seven mourning days in his chair, wrapped in his grief. He received his acquaintances with a nod, and the strangers with a bat of an eyelid.

"I did not know that my wife and children knew so many people," he told himself in a moment of benevolence.

Hannah, silent and drained, divided her time between sitting by her husband as expected, and in solitude in the bedroom with her friends from the village.

"Do not worry," they told her. "Shmuel is taking care of everything."

"But I didn't know that the rabbi has so many fans and my children so many friends..." she whispered.

Shmuel did take care of everything. He made sure that there would be refreshments for the visitors, that the tea pot would always be full, and all while adhering to the rules of mourning, which included, among other things, three prayers a day and reading Psalms.

Good women brought refreshments and food throughout the day, and prayer books were brought from the synagogue nearby. From time-to-time Shmuel felt the curious glances staring at his black beard and the large yarmulke on his head.

He divided his time among the familiar and foreign acquaintances, including his friends from when he was growing up in the village. And these were not many. They were ten friends from the village who studied together in Rosh Pina until he transferred to the yeshiva in Jerusalem. Three of them made sure to visit him on each of the seven days of mourning.

One of the three moved to Rosh Pina and ran a cardboard packaging business there. The other two remained in Yesodot and continued the family tradition of growing fruit trees in orchards around the village. The other, Yehuda, was even elected to chair the local council.

"Don't wait for the others," he told him on one of his visits. "Three out of the group left the country a long time ago, and apart from Hagai, who sends Happy New Year letters once every two years, we have no contact with any of them. Two others, unfortunately, died of various diseases, not the fever but other ailments the world has to offer. And Avi, who had always been a little strange, disappeared into one of the caves in the Meron area and does not want contact with humanity. Yes, humanity includes his parents. I told you there are more ailments in the world."

On another day of the Shiva,[10] Yehuda dragged him to the row of the Washingtonian trees outside the house, where they sat on an old wooden bench, breathed in some air, ate a piece of pie, and washed it down with hot tea.

"I didn't know that my father had so many fans," Shmuel told him after swallowing and drinking, pointing to the incessant stream of visitors.

"Do not be naïve." Yehuda chuckled. "A large portion of them are trying to kill two birds with one stone."

"I don't understand." Shmuel gave him a puzzled look.

"What's there to understand?" Yehuda grinned. "Your family has become the story of the month through the Galilee, and you should know that not much happens around these areas. It is quite boring here. Some of those present at the funeral came to see how a Christian priest is buried in a Jewish cemetery, while another priest recites all the other traditional Jewish prayers."

Shmuel lowered his eyes.

"But don't worry, many others, like me for example, come out of respect, appreciation, and participation in mourning. Are you really not a Christian anymore?"

"The answer is yes. We'll talk more. I need to get back inside; prayers are about to begin."

***

---

10. **Shiva** is the week-long mourning period in Judaism for first-degree relatives.

Throughout the Shiva, Shmuel had no real contact with his sister, Esther. Taking care of everything and concern for his parents took up most of his time. Every day, after the last of the visitors had gone, the members of the household fell exhausted on their beds and into a frantic night's sleep.

From time to time one of the women of the village turned to him and complained that Esther ignored her and would rather shut herself in her room than accept her consolation. Shmuel heard but did not listen. He, too, would sometimes prefer to be alone in his pain rather than hear the same consoling words over and over again.

On the seventh day of the Shiva, after the evening prayer that closed the days of mourning, Shmuel sat down with his parents for more moments of silence. At his mother's request, he turned to Esther's room and invited her to join the family.

Esther got out of bed and with hesitant steps joined the table. Shmuel looked at her out of the corner of his eye, seeing the horrifying image of his mother on her anguish and grief.

Shmuel knew the effects of time, he felt the signs on himself as well, but something in Esther bothered him considerably.

About three decades had passed since he left his home on a journey of several days to bring Dudi home. The image of Esther as it was saved in his memory since they parted ways, accompanied him over the years and instilled in him pride and longing.

Graceful and glowing with a captivating smile and blue eyes, the girl gave him a strong hug and whispered to him, "Come back quickly, we miss you."

When he returned eight days prior, after sharing hugs, kisses, and tears with his parents, he turned to his sister for a long embrace, yet her eyes dropped from his gaze. She was not the same Esther, he told himself. On all seven days they barely exchanged two, perhaps three words.

When his exhausted parents retired to their room, the brother and sister remained sitting in silence around the table.

"Let's go out to the bench, we need fresh air." He put his hand on her arm and led or maybe even slightly pulled her to their childhood bench near the row of palm trees.

"It's difficult," he told her. "Though I didn't know just how hard." He tried to break the wall of silence.

Quiet minutes passed and suddenly Esther raised her head, sent a blue gaze directly at him and said in a broken voice, "I killed Dudi."

The same sky that dropped on him when he saw his brother being pulled to his death, collapsed again into the abyss.

"No," he said trying to stay composed. "You didn't kill him. The murderers who blew the hotel up killed him. I was there."

Esther gave her brother a strange look, one he had never seen in her eyes or even in the eyes of anyone else. She put her hand on his arm and pulled him to the dairy next to the house. A pleasant breeze blew in as she opened the door, and a faint light coming from the house illuminated the dairy.

"Here, look," she told him. "The milk jugs are gone." And immediately crumpled to her knees, whimpering, and screaming from the depths of her heart.

Shmuel knelt beside her and hugged her shoulders, trying to calm her trembling body. The uncontrollable tremor passed from his sister to him. A sense of helplessness enveloped him. The milk jugs he remembered from the dairy became strangely threatening, menacing demons.

His attempt to reassure his sister and calm himself down had failed. He finally hugged her, and with great effort picked her up from the dairy floor and carried her into the house.

She did not utter a word. She closed herself in her room and refused to see Shmuel or her parents.

After forty-eight hours of confinement, Hannah invited Yocheved, a forty-year-old single woman, who was known as the village therapist. She entered Esther's room, and after a long hour of unsuccessful attempts to get her to talk, she left the room and shared her diagnosis, "This is normal after the trauma following a deep mental crisis. She will recover from grieving her brother and will be fine. She needs her time." She looked at Shmuel.

After another day of confinement, Hannah entered her daughter's room holding a bowl of chicken soup. To the mother's delight, Esther sipped a few tablespoons and whispered to her, "Send Shmuel in."

Red-eyed, pale, and worried, Shmuel entered his sister's room. She was wearing the same clothes she did that day at the dairy, though they seemed slightly larger. On her trousers, there were still dirt stains from her kneeling, and her body was desperate for a good shower.

Without saying a word, she picked up the crumpled, tear-soaked pillow that was under her head, and with a weak, trembling hand pulled out a "Davar,"[11] a newspaper she had hidden under it and handed it to her brother.

The headline read in large letters: "The KING DAVID HOTEL IN JERUSALEM WAS BLOWN UP BY THE

---

11. **Davar** is the Hebrew-language daily newspaper published in the British Mandate of Palestine.

IRGUN[12] MEMBERS, WHO INSERTED EXPLOSIVES INSIDE MILK JUGS BROUGHT TO THE BASEMENT OF THE HOTEL'S SOUTH WING."

Shmuel was in shock. Lost for words, he kissed his sister on the forehead and went out to the bench.

After a few minutes she went and sat down next to him. In silence, they sat there holding hands, as they did decades before, looking at the snow-capped peak of Mount Hermon that could be seen from a great distance.

The shared secret benefited them both. Shmuel burned the "Davar" newspaper from July 1946 behind the dairy, and since then, they did not exchange a single word. Not about the newspaper and certainly not about the King David Hotel. They had drowned it all in the abyss of oblivion. At least so they thought.

Esther returned to work as a sewing teacher at the "Bnot Yaakov" school for girls in the village, and Shmuel accompanied his father to the synagogue and to Torah studies.

***

After days of anguish and mourning, Shmuel travelled to Safed, rented a room not far from the synagogue named

---

12. **The Irgun** (Etzel) was a Zionist paramilitary organization that operated in Mandate Palestine between 1931 and 1948.

after the holy ARI,[13] and spent his days in prayer, self-reflection, in a quest to build harmony and peace with his God. On one morning of deep contemplation, the rabbi of a nearby synagogue came knocking on his door.

"I was asked to let you know that your father died in his sleep."

That same night, the rabbi was buried by his son, Dudi. When the Shiva had ended, the council, led by its chairperson Yehuda, appeared at the house.

"We have come to offer you to the position of village rabbi," Yehuda and his friends told him, looking at Shmuel with eyes full of expectations.

"Why me?" Shmuel asked humbly.

"Because you are the rabbi's son," they replied.

"That's not enough," Shmuel protested. "Besides, I was a Christian for thirty years."

"True," they replied. "But we view that as an advantage. You have seen everything, and your desire to be a Jew comes out of real choice and not out of birth or habit."

"That's actually true..." he murmured.

"We heard you pray and there's no one else like you. We are confident you will make an excellent rabbi."

---

13. **Isaac ben Solomon Luria Ashkenazi**, commonly known as "Ha'ARI," was a leading rabbi and Jewish mystic in the community of Safed in the 16th century.

"With God's help." Shmuel bowed his head in humble acceptance.

Not many days passed, and a new sign was put up on the front door:

"Shmuel Meisels"
Village Rabbi
Son of Rabbi Shlomo Meisels, Of Blessed Memory

***

Her father's death added to Esther's agony. Even her brother's appointment as his successor could not alleviate her grief and loneliness. The turning point came about a month later. An agent came to her home and invited her to a meeting at the organization's headquarters in the "Yemenite Vineyard" neighborhood in Tel Aviv.

To the amazement of her mother and brother, she accepted the invitation without hesitation, stepped into the shower, changed her clothes, packed several items in a small bag, and said goodbye to them.

The neighborhood was located in south Tel Aviv, had remained true to its name. After the founding of Tel Aviv in 1909, one of the city's respectable lords bought land south of the city, in the area between the new Hebrew town and Arab Jaffa.

According to the laws of those days, the Ottoman government was allowed to expropriate any area of land that remained desolate for a period exceeding three years. In order to overcome this decree, the landowner decided to plant a vineyard instead. Later, Jews from Yemen began to arrive establishing a neighborhood for the new immigrants, that became known as the "Yemenite Vineyard."[14]

The Irgun chose to establish its headquarters in this neighborhood despite its proximity to Arab Jaffa, as its crowded houses and narrow streets would prevent British armored vehicles from entering to search for members of the underground.

Shortly after the British left Israel, the Irgun had decided that its first overt action would be to seize Jaffa. For this purpose, the organization rallied hundreds of its members from all over the country, including Esther, the warrior from Yesodot.

Preparations for war had been completed and Esther was tasked with acting as a liaison between the forces deployed in the tactical assembly areas throughout neighborhood.

---

14. The Yemenite Vineyard is known in Hebrew as 'Kerem HaTeymanim.'

"This is an important role bearing grave responsibility," the commander explained to her. "It is not always possible or necessary to rely solely on a wireless communication."

Esther gladly accepted the mission assigned to her. She restored all of her energy and was prepared for the war ahead.

***

Muhammad Salameh's friends called him the "Hawk Eye." He carried a sniper rifle, and when he was not busy shooting Jews, he used to go to the dunes south of Jaffa to hunt partridges and hares. His friends would say that woe to the hare who would dare peek its whiskers from its burrow as they would surely be doomed.

From time to time he would fulfill his national duty by going to Hassan Beck Mosque to shoot at a careless Jew walking the southern streets of Tel Aviv. The Hassan Beck Mosque was built in 1916, by order of the Turkish military governor of those days, and upon its completion received his name.

The mosque was built in the north of Jaffa with intent to mark the border between Arab Jaffa and Hebrew Tel Aviv, thus preventing the spread of the Jewish city to the south toward Jaffa. The mosque boasted a tall spire, and narrow, winding internal stairs that led to its summit.

Only two people would use the stairs. One was the muezzin, who had to go all the way up five times a day for the call to prayer. The other, was Muhammad Salameh.

One day, Muhammad "Hawk Eye" Salameh was called to the Qadi of Jaffa, who also served as the spiritual leader of the Arab forces.

"I heard that the Jews are about to raid Jaffa. You are the only one who can help. I ask that you go up to the mosque and make them think again..."

Muhammad climbed the tower with his sniper rifle. From above he noticed a great deal of military movement. He was looking for a worthy target. Between the cracks of a stone wall built by the Jews to protect them from snipers and stone hurlers, he waited for an appropriate target. After half an hour of anticipation, he noticed a blonde woman rushing between the gaps. He tensed, and rested his finger on the trigger, waiting for his victim like an eagle on its prey.

Minutes passed before he noticed the woman retracing her steps. A split second was enough for him. He pulled the trigger and saw the woman fall as a one inch diameter bullet left a gaping hole in her temple.

**

All of the residents of Yesodot attended the funeral.

An honorary guard fired salutes in tribute of the heroine that had fallen.

Esther was buried next to her beloved brother, Dudi.

At the end of the thirty days of mourning, a shared monument was placed on both of their tombs, reading the words:

"Reed and Rush Shall Decay"
Isaiah 19:6

Printed in Great Britain
by Amazon

38640511R00155